About the Author

Adrian Wright is the acclaimed author of several biographies including the life of L P Hartley *Foreign Country*, the life of John Lehmann *A Pagan Adventure*, the life of William Alwyn *The Innumerable Dance*, and a collection of theatre pieces *No Laughing Matter*. His three books on British musical theatre, *A Tanner's Worth of Tune*, *West End Broadway* and *Must Close Saturday*, are standard works, and his survey of British musical films *Cheer Up!* is published in 2020. His fiction includes the novel *Maroon*, and two of his 'Francis and Gordon Jones' series, *The Voice of Doom* and *The Coming Day*. He lives in Norfolk.

FORGET ME NOT

ADRIAN WRIGHT

Matador
9 Priory Business Park,
Wistow Road, Kibworth Beauchamp,
Leicestershire. LE8 0RX
Tel: 0116 279 2299
Email: books@troubador.co.uk
Web: www.troubador.co.uk/matador
Twitter: @matadorbooks

ISBN 978 1838593 131

British Library Cataloguing in Publication Data.
A catalogue record for this book is available from the British Library.

Printed and bound in the UK by TJ International, Padstow, Cornwall
Typeset in 11pt Adobe Garamond Pro by Troubador Publishing Ltd, Leicester, UK

Matador is an imprint of Troubador Publishing Ltd

MIX
Paper from
responsible sources
FSC® C013056

for Stephen Boswell

'Say hello to pretty Lily
When you see her in the 'dilly
For she's the little donor I adore
There's not a finer filly
Than Piccadilly Lily
A masher couldn't want for any more.
You may dream through life
Of a girl beyond compare
With eyes that have more pep than piccalilli,
On a pudding she's the custard
She's as hot as Colman's Mustard
None other than the Lil of Piccadilly!'

(H. Baynes and Reginald Seamore, 1907)

Note

Words taken from Victorian and Edwardian music-hall songs
are used throughout the text

PROLOGUE
1910

I

'Sing us one of the old songs, George!'

'Let the chorus go!'

'Yes, George, try old man. Do what you can. We can't forget what you used to be in the days when life was new. Sing us a song!'

'If you go wrong, we'll help to pull you through!'

While London sleeps, and all the lamps are gleaming, millions of its people now lie sweetly dreaming. Some have no homes, and o'er their sorrows weep. Oh, it's all right in the summertime. In the summertime it's lovely. Others laugh and play the game while London's fast asleep.

George is playing the game right enough, leaning on Gertie in an alley off the Strand at the rear end of the Adelphi, togged up like a toff, puffing at a cigar and boasting of his royal connections with his flies open.

'I know the Emperor of Japan.'

Gertie and the others (Flo, two dancers from the Metropolitan and one of the lah-dee-dah boys from the Empire) try not to encourage him.

'Very likely,' says Gertie.

1

'I've had cigars and ginger ale with the Duke of Baden Baden and the Prince of Wales. He's a bosom friend of mine.'

George does the wobbley walk he does in Margate when he's on the prom, as if he's as nancy as any of the genuine nancy boys and off he goes about how he likes to be beside the seaside where the brass bands play. The Strand might as well be the front at Worthing the way he goes on.

'If Margate were down in Regent Street,' says George, 'and the Isle of Man were somewhere down the Strand, wouldn't it be grand, listening to the band! If Brighton fair were in Trafalgar Square, Piccadilly all surrounded by the sea, and you could bathe with all the girls down Bond Street – what a grand place London Town would be.'

The curtain's down at the old Mo, the girls at the Trocadero peek from the top windows of their dressing-rooms, tippy-toed on ballerina legs to see if Stage Door Johnnies are at the Stage Door where Stage Door Johnnies should be. They point and whisper and giggle and decide which shall be theirs. The pretty heads draw back from the windows when they catch the cries from below.

'We'll have oysters and wine at two a.m., two a.m., two a.m.! Oysters and wine at two a.m.!'

There's a crowd of them, tipsy-elbowed, heading for the Cri, passing by the gulley that lets in to the alley, when George and Flo and the nancy boys rush out into the Strand almost into the arms of the seekers of oysters and wine at whatever hour. They cry out at each other as old friends, colliding strangers uncertain of where they might be headed. The Cri or the public house? The brothel or the back passage? Their legs mish-mash, the thighs of the nancy boys shining in neatly pleated trousers, Gertie pouting and winking the other eye at the prospect of better things to become of the night, Flo lifting her skirt above her ankle as she slides against the toff who with luck might take her back to the Albany for an aristocratic deflowering.

Of course, it's George who links their arms together, gathers up their bodies and leads them on. So they all walk the wibbley wobbley walk, and they all talk the wibbley wobbley talk, they all smile the wibbley wobbley smile when the day is dawning. Then all through the wibbley wobbley walk, they get a wibbley wobbley feeling in the morning.

The cut runs down Villiers Street towards the Thames. Something slightly mystical gives them pause as they see ahead the slope running to the Embankment, as if the murky water were calling them. The shared pursuit of happiness stills, their voices soft now, as if a temple has sprung up invisible around them.

'Or there's Hattie Prince at the Tivoli!'

They heard the voice, never knowing where it came from, but there can be no doubt.

'Oh yes! Hattie at the Tivoli! The Tivoli! The Tivoli!'

It's not a decision they'll regret, although Flo and the Empire boys had been hoping for a night off from fairyland, and George is past it, supposedly headed for stardom in another theatrical sphere, but the thought of Hattie, resplendently masculine, pulls them on.

'I want to sing in opera!' George shouts, but nobody's listening much. 'I've got that kind of voice!'

It's a frog's, really and truly, but Flo's too kind to say.

'What kind of voice have you got, George?' asks someone, spluttering because of the drink and wanting to lead him on.

'I'd always sing in opera if I could have my choice.'

George is underneath the lamplight's glitter, his throat open like a nightingale's.

'Signor Caruso told me I ought to do so, that's why I want to sing in…'

And then he's away. Trilling.

'Op-op-op-op-era!' he sings, letting the falsetto airs into the soft night.

II

Oh, England is thriving!

Selfridges has a shop in London, Woolworths has opened its first store in Liverpool, no less than the King and Queen have opened the Victoria and Albert Museum. It's the year of Halley's Comet, dangling somewhere infinitesimal above Edwardian London. The stories of a foreigner called Balzac are denounced as mucky reading and seized by the police. Another foreigner, Guglielmo Marconi, has invented a thing called the wireless telegraph, which will play a part in the capture of an infamous Edwardian murderer and his mistress. On 5 May, Edward VII, wearying of his very own era, insists 'I shall not give in. I shall go on' and dies the next day. Miners, possibly ignorant of the serene image of Edwardian England, strike for an eight-hour day. Within weeks, Charles Rolls, the first British man to cross the Channel in a British aeroplane, gains new fame as the first British man to be killed in a British aeroplane. Arty types flock to the Grafton Galleries for Roger Fry's exhibition of post-impressionism. Those who appreciate more hearty diversion lament the death of Lottie Collins, destined for music-hall immortality.

A gramophone company has expressed interest in making a recording of Belle Elmore's 'She Never Went Further Than That', but thinks better of it after listening to its suggestive lyrics. The papers say that theatre is dead, as if only the year before Maud Allan hadn't got into the headlines with her scandalous Salome at the Palace Theatre, but now the Palace is showing Kinemacolor films between the music-hall turns, and people are beginning to prefer the Kinemacolor. Is music-hall dying? Never! Marie Lloyd's still doing the rounds of the halls although she's got the most appalling cough and oh, the innuendo.

Mrs Ormiston Chant wants the halls closed. 'Lead us not into temptation,' she insists, 'but do away with the foul spots where temptation exists. Sweep them away and London shall be happier and England better, free from the horrid slavery so many poor women are bound to.'

Imagine what Marie, if bowdlerized, would say of Mrs Chant and her crew. They're a somewhat of a rum lot, well, the best thing I can say, is pom-tiddley-om-pom-pom-pom-pom, tiddley-om-pom-pom-pom-pay! In an attempt to realign Britain's reputation for respectability, the Girl Guides Association is born.

Oh, the halls are packed, but already the writing's getting itself ready to write on the wall. What's the use of asking everybody to all go down the Strand when Gatti's in Villiers Street has turned into a cinema?

Belle asks the same question, sounding a warning to a just-begun 1910, despite those music-hall songs that still stir audiences at the Hippodromes. Not that she's given up hope. Belle could still make it big, with the right song, being in the perfect place at the God-given time. She has the talent, needs the luck. The chocolate coloured coon G H Elliott is made for life with 'I Used To Sigh For The Silvery Moon', Hetty King is rumoured to have only paid a few coppers for the rights to sing 'All The Nice Girls Love A Sailor' but every barrow boy down Hampstead way whistles it, and sailors, in or out of someone's arms, embrace it as their own, Gertie Gitana is passing herself off as 'Queen of the Cannibal Isle', Wilkie Bard (chronically unfunny as ever) is rolling them in the aisles with 'I Can Say Truly Rural' and laughing all the way to several banks.

As it is, Belle's making do with one of her old numbers, 'Down Lover's Walk', a location to which audiences seem reluctant to accompany her. She's had no bookings since October, and the hope of Fairy Queen at the Drury Lane pantomime had come to nothing, although they'd asked her to do charity work for the Music-Hall Ladies Guild.

It was kind of the Guild to suggest her for an honorary office; one that kept her offstage. She was vaguely aware of being considered an object of pity by her performing colleagues, but she saw how this might signal the end of a career that had proceeded only in jerks and shudders. Change was in the air, and something had to be done. Just before Christmas, she'd been to the Charing Cross Bank, intending to withdraw both her personal savings and the £270 in the account she shared with her husband. Peter knew nothing about the £200 she had in the Birkbeck Bank, so it could stay where it was for the present. He'd never been good with money. Since leaving America, his business life was as unpredictable as a game of snakes and ladders; currently, he earned a living as a dentist to whom patients might submit themselves with no fear of pain. All that talk about him making a fortune out of 'Ohrsorb' but she couldn't remember, not ever listening attentively when he

6

spoke, whether it was a lotion or suppository. Did you put the stuff on or up? Anyway, it had come to nothing, no matter where people put it.

On a personal, as well as professional, level, Peter had little to offer, but she had always attracted male admirers. The German students she and Peter took in as lodgers at Hilldrop Crescent were fine examples of their race. Men had always been drawn to her. A pity no one had written a song called 'Moths To A Flame'; she'd have sung that with conviction. More than one of the gallery boys at the music-halls had been bewitched when she sang, or when she emerged from the stage door, plump and over all perfumed and full-lipped. Get 1910 over, and she'd be off, ready for it now, older and wiser. It wasn't until she'd left the Charing Cross Bank that the manager's words hit her.

'Regretfully, madam, the terms of your agreement with the bank cannot be overlooked. One year's notice is required on accounts of this type. If you wish to give notice today, that would be quite in order, but I'm afraid our rules cannot allow ...'

Sod that! Another year? A whole year before she could get at the money! She was sick to the stomach, cheated. But she remembered the jewels. No bank would ever get its hands on them. It cheered her up, knowing she had the jewels to depend on. She had been in her element at the Music-Hall Ladies Guild Christmas party for widows and orphans of fellow artistes, dolling herself up until she truly resembled the Belle of the ball, the flash of her marquise wedding ring glittering as she handed out the jellies to the little dears, her diamond earrings swaying miniature chandeliers above the trembling trifles, her diamond tiara brooch (a step too far, one or two of the Music-Hall ladies suggested) and the brilliant 'rising sun' brooch, glimpsed by many a child that afternoon as it caught their unbelieving eyes, and never forgotten. Of course, there were other jewels that never saw the light of day, that Peter knew nothing of, jewels much too ostentatious and extravagant for a childrens' party, jewels that she would not wear even for a ball, and now, now that she knew her money was locked away from her, the jewels would be her way out. Nevertheless, she wished she had not seen the text Peter (for who else might it have been?) had put into her handbag.

In that day the Lord will take away the bravery of their tinkling ornaments about their feet ... the bonnets, and the ornaments of the legs, and the headbands, and the tablets, and the earrings, the rings, and nose jewels ... the mantles, and the wimples, and the crisping pins, the glasses, and the fine linen, and the hoods and the veils, and it shall come to pass, that instead of a sweet smell there shall be stink.

III

Coincidence, all too often used in the feeblest and most patently cobbled-together novels, played its part that day, on the afternoon of 31 January 1910, in what would in its way be both a beginning and an end.

Ethel Braund, twenty-five and a milliner at one of London's lesser known department stores, left work as usual at six o'clock and made her way to Charing Cross, where she had arranged to meet her aunt who was travelling from Dollis Hill. Aunt and niece would have a light supper at Lyons Corner House, and speak of family matters, including the death of Ethel's uncle from natural causes only a week or so before. Neither of them having a close affinity to the late departed, the solemn content would soon be dispensed with, and refreshment begun. Unknown to Ethel, her unmarried aunt, Emilia Dewsbury, had entered their appointment wrongly in her diary, and the very next day would be waiting at Lyons Corner House at the very same time for the arrival of her niece. Since Miss Dewsbury could not afford the telephone, it was two days later that the confusion was explained to the satisfaction of both parties.

Ethel waited across the street for half an hour, keeping an eye out. It was a cold night, with frost promised. She pulled fast the fur of her tippet, thankful for the kid leather gloves she had purchased, at her usual ten per cent off, from the store in which she worked, and the wool coat that had served her already for long years. Her feet grew numb. It seemed pointless to wait outside any longer. Perhaps, after all, her aunt was already inside, warming herself and toying with a menu.

The temperature was almost tropical, misting her vision as Ethel found the appropriate room and the area where she and her aunt usually sat. Her heart sank as she surveyed the diners, among whom there were probably a fair number of spinster aunts, but not the one Ethel required. The place was crowded, every table taken so far as Ethel could see, not a seat to be had. She wished now she had turned heel and made her way home, but it was too late, and though the smell of food made her slightly nauseous, she felt the need to sit down, reminded of a nagging discomfort from the dental extraction she had undergone a few days earlier. She rubbed a smudge of 'Bolton's Arithmetical Comforter' on her gums when no one was looking. The smell was disgusting, and the ointment left a burning sensation for a few moments. That, thought Ethel, must be it doing me good. A dab of the stuff had got into her eye. Through the fog, she was vaguely aware of someone calling across the floor, a jewelled hand fluttering from deep within the room.

'Excuse me, miss.'

It was a nippy. Ethel recognised her from other visits, a fresh-faced girl, impeccable in what after all was effectively a theatrical costume.

'Were you wanting a seat? Only, the lady over there says you're welcome to join her if you wish.'

The hand was waggling at her again, a distant light waved from shore, from a corner near a potted palm, and Ethel, her feet starting to thaw, her hands ready for gliding out of the ten-per-cent-off kid gloves bought with her staff account, followed the nippy to the far-off table. Was this wise of Ethel? The woman whose hand is no longer waggling but stretching up to greet her as if she were a long-lost friend, is not the sort with whom Ethel normally associates, looks the type of woman who would be out of place in a Baptist chapel, a woman from whom the world had all too obviously withheld no bodily pleasure.

'Well, dearie, come and join us!' cries Belle Elmore. 'Welcome to Harmony Hall! You look frozen up. Give the girl some tea, miss, for God's sake.'

Ethel is glad to sit down, the weight taken off her feet. Her vision starts to clear. The woman is stout, and colourful, and loud. She glimmers at the wrists, in her ears, at her neck, and the features of her face reside behind a cloud of powder and artificial reinforcement. This may have been a mistake, thinks Ethel, but she's here now, and no one from the chapel is likely to see her, and it's a relief to set down her handbag, a stout piece of equipment and surprisingly heavy for a milliner at one of London's lesser-known department stores, but inside it is *Climbing to Righteousness* by the Reverend Archibald Purchase (retired), unnecessarily weighty because he insisted on its publication in two volumes instead of one. Ethel feels the lighter for having set her handbag down, and slides it deeply beneath the table.

Belle's voice, theatrically projected, dominated the room. Two young lovers fled almost as soon as Ethel arrived. A man with a bowler hat by his plate gave up his anchovies on toast, leaving behind what must have been an almost complete pot of tea. When the nippy turned away, Belle snatched it from the table and began pouring a cup for her unexpected guest. As Belle's faintly American twang bounced around the sugar bowls and china and tinkled the gas fittings, the place emptied. People sensed there was no point in staying if they were to retain what hope they had entered the room with, knew that the florid woman was one of those who used up all the air around her, sucked the life out of their lungs, lessened the meaning of their lives. Her blouse, florid and meticulously loosened at the edges, bloomed out and in, folds of pink flesh breaking through. For much of the time, Belle made as if she was about to leave on urgent business, but never went.

'Much as I'd like to dawdle, dear, I'm third turn at the Camberwell Empire. What a dive! Not what I'm used to, dear, but needs must at times. Fanny Robina is second on. Poor Fanny. Died the death last night with her new song. "Dear Mother I've Come Home To Die". It made me die, anyway! Tears of laughter, mind you, dear. I said to the manager "How the hell do you expect me to follow a bloody misery guts like her?" By the time I went on several patrons had vacated the theatre and thrown themselves off the nearest bridge, they was so depressed. Too much Fanny if you ask me. I mean, Fanny Leslie's doing her "A Polish Girl's The Girl For Me", so the followers of Lesbos will be queuing up for it tonight. I discourage them, dear. Can't do with all those corsets and hooks and eyes to undo, but I can always find time for a Stage Door Johnny or two.' She stopped talking long enough to put in a startlingly strong wink.

'Pass us your cup, dear. I open up too easily, that's my trouble and no two ways about it, I open up like a great blooming floribunda rose on a sunny incline in its first flush. No sooner I've met someone than I fling open the door to my inner sanctum. The door's wedged open, dear. That's my philosophy. If you're Irish, come into the parlour, except I'm Polish, of course! Are you married, dear?'

From being cold, Ethel was now beginning to feel hot under the collar.

'I see you're not, dear.' Belle leaned across the teapot to whisper. 'The virginal glow. You can always tell. I mean, we've all been there, haven't we, if only temporarily!'

She let out a roar that turned heads away from plates of fancies.

'You get a frowsty crowd here, dear. Like to give the impression they've never wiped their own bottoms.'

Ethel forced a smile, thinking of advice that might be given for just such an uncomfortable occasion by the Reverend Purchase, but Belle's voice had moved on.

'Like I said, I told him "One last heave-ho, dear,"' and for a moment Ethel thinks the woman is talking of the Revd Purchase, but of course it's a husband she's conjured up.

'"One great effort for old England", I told him. I mean, it's come to something when you have to appeal to their patriotic streak, but Peter couldn't do it, dear, unable to rise to the occasion. Didn't know where to put my eyes and that's the truth. What was worse was that I had that song of Millie Payne's on my mind, and I could scarcely stop myself from singing it out loud right there and then. "Has Anybody Seen My Tiddler?". I subdued it, dear, kept it to myself, being the wisest option when the object of concern is there in front of you and doing nothing out of the ordinary as you might say unless you had a magnifying glass. I tried staring at it, mesmerising, like the Arabs do with cobras in baskets, but nothing happened. Still, I hummed it, dear, hummed the tune, which he may have recognised or he may not. Didn't know and didn't much care to be honest with you. Hummed it, and whistled it too, to cover up the French for embarrassment.'

This Ethel, Ethel Braund, unaware of the elephant in the room named Ethel le Neve, feels robbed of her own person by this woman, almost pinches herself under the table to remind herself that she is Ethel Braund, employed as a milliner off Regent Street, out on her weekly treat at Lyons Corner House. Her life, until she sat at this table because there was no other space in the room and had been invited to join its occupant, had been blameless. If it hadn't been for the meeting with this stranger, it would have gone on just as innocently for the rest of her days, spent trimming hats that she occasionally recognised as her own bobbing along Piccadilly. Where did you get that hat? Oh, the girls at the buzzy sewing machines and sneezing among the feathers broke out at once. Where did you get that hat? Where did you get that tile? Isn't it a nobby one, and quite the latest style. I should like to have one, just the same as that. Where'ere I go they shout 'Hello! Where did you get that hat?'.

There's no end to the facts that Belle lays out for Ethel's delight, not much of which Ethel will remember in future days or years. In fact, forty seven years later, Ethel will recall one thing, almost, perhaps, word for word, that Belle said across the table at Lyons Corner House.

'I know I'm wasting my time working for the Music-Hall Ladies Guild,' she said. 'All those old cats, you wouldn't believe it! They'll be the death of me, dear, honest they will.'

In that, at least, Belle Elmore, alias Cora Turner, alias Kunigunde Mackamotzki, alias Mrs Hawley Harvey Crippen, was wrong.

IV

Two weeks before Ethel's meeting with her, Belle's disruptive behaviour had so wearied her husband that he decided something must be done. As a qualified doctor – perhaps not as qualified as the certificates awarded him by certain dubious American institutions suggested – it was only natural he should seek a way out of what are discreetly described as marital difficulties. He might more sensibly have paid a visit to a Mrs Hicks, who dispensed helpful medications from a shady hovel off Clerkenwell Road. Ada Hicks was well known for supplying opiates and other medical niceties under the counter, with not too many questions asked, and no forms to be filled in. For some reason, on this occasion Belle's husband took the official line, and on 17 January 1910 visited the firm of Lewis and Burrows, where he asked for five grains of hydrobromide of hyoscine.

It may be that Messrs Lewis and Burrows were at lunch or in the laboratory when he called, for they would surely have questioned his request. Well known to them as a regular customer he might be, but they would almost certainly have raised an eyebrow. The young assistant who at that moment represented Messrs Lewis and Burrows raised his own eyebrow, peered at the label of the bottle and asked 'Five?'

Yes, replied Doctor Crippen, five grains. He didn't wait for the boy to enquire further.

'I'm well aware that a quarter of a grain is quite enough to cause death in humans,' he said. 'As you know, I have frequently had use of it, albeit in smaller quantities, for dental purposes. On this occasion, it's rats.'

'Oh, I see,' said the boy, already wrapping the purchase. 'Rats!'

'A plague of them. And associated vermin.'

'They're right little blighters, aren't they half? The very thing, sir. You'll sign the book?'

It was as well for justice that he did; Crippen's signature paved another step to the execution shed.

1957

CHAPTER ONE

'I can remember when they used to line up out there, a queue of them winding. Poverty Corner, they called it.'

'Not the big names, though?' said Glynis. 'Not the Marie Lloyds?'

Standing at the window looking down into the Waterloo Road, Monty Desmond looked the harder just to be sure.

'I'm talking forty, fifty years ago,' he said, tweaking the blind back into position. 'There were the music-halls to be filled. There's never been a time like it.'

He'd stubbed out his cigar (success and reputation had moved him on from Player's Weights) and started another. Glynis was sitting the other side of his desk, her legs crossed, her dress ending well below the knee, a pencil and pad, hoping to look professional. She'd been warned. Monty Desmond had a reputation. Ten years ago, at what had passed for the job interview, she'd mentioned her association with an Irish convent to be on the safe side and he hadn't lifted an eyebrow. She hadn't had him down for good behaviour, gave herself a couple of weeks before she up and left, but he'd surprised her.

'Do you ever wonder,' she said, 'where people go?'

'What?'

'Where do they go? The forgotten people. Where do they go? Do you never wonder?'

'I'll tell you something,' he said, and he was standing with his back to the window, silhouetted against the early evening light that had crept around a corner.

'And you'll think I've gone soft,' he warned her, but she was used to it. 'Wherever I am, I'm thinking of them. The forgotten ones. I've always wanted to turn a corner and bump into one of them.'

'Well, now's your chance.'

'No. It won't work.'

'Why not? What've you got to lose?'

He had to admit that Glynis had a point. Anyway, it was her idea and she wasn't going to let go of it. It had been years since Monty had presented a provincial variety show. As for doing it on a pier! Concert party stuff, he'd say, crap he'd left behind long ago, at Skegness or Bournemouth or, a graveyard if you were a comic, Southwold.

Monty's lucky break had come when he signed up an American singer for cabaret at the Dorchester. He'd worked alongside Ted Grant, a business partner who had persuaded a disorientated Judy Garland to do a week at the Pigalle, so he owed Grant one hell of a favour that Grant now wanted to call in. Grant had signed a contract for a two-week booking to follow the summer show at the fag end of the season on the north coast of Norfolk, but he'd got into a financial tangle with another project and wanted Monty to bail him out. It might mean some sort of co-production between them, with Monty putting the show together and taking the lion's share of the takings. Time was short. The show had to be announced by the end of May, and it was already the end of March.

'So, take me through it again,' said Monty. His hands were splayed at the back of his head.

'I've looked at what Ted has planned for the summer show,' said Glynis. 'It's standard seaside stuff, half way between concert party and a pierrot troupe.'

'Oh, God. Glynis, it's washed up.'

'Hmm. No star names, anyway. It is Cromer, after all. And on the end of a pier. It's not the Palladium.'

'It's not even Sparrow's Nest at Lowestoft. So why should we be even thinking about this?'

'You know why. You owe Ted big time. I don't think you'll lose on it. He's been good to you, compared to some you've worked with. Why not leave it to me? Let me see what I can do.'

Monty doesn't answer, leaves the room. There's always a telephone call to be made, a call to be taken. Max Bygraves is a pain in the arse, Winnie Atwell's got arthritis in her fingers, sailor-boy Trevor Stanford is thinking of changing his name to Russ Conway and has just written a musical for Frankie Howerd, Peter Brough wants a year away from Archie Andrews, some crackpot wants to put tap-dancing on radio, and an even more cracked pot has turned *Mrs Dale's Diary* into a musical.

Monty's right, of course. Glynis was always the outsider, didn't know a thing before Monty took her on. Not her fault. She's Irish, for God's sake. Alone, Glynis treats the quiet moment as hers. She stands at the window, looking out.

So that's Poverty Corner, not even ghosts lining up to see what's going on. In the street, there's no-one that isn't a passer-by, where once the people from the halls waited, hoping for a booking, a week at the Wood Green Empire, grateful for a split week at the Northampton New and the Stepney Paragon, jugglers, acrobats, singers, conjurors, speciality cyclists, Flags of All Nations, tableaux vivants, dog acts, ballerinas, white eyed kaffirs, coster comics, cockney comics, Irish comics, eccentric comics, never known to make a cat laugh comics, siffleurs, negro delineators, amputees, male impersonators, female impersonators, coon singers, minstrel troupes, cross-talk duos, child singers, illusionists, escapologists, card manipulators, ventriloquists, equilibrists, pantomimists, hypnotists, writers, musicians, midgets, dwarves, seals playing the drums, chimpanzees riding tricycles, paper tearers. She'd once seen Monty tear a paper-tearer to shreds. He said you just couldn't get the paper.

It's a world gone by, but why shouldn't it happen again, as it once had for those people queuing around Poverty Corner as far as the eye could see, anything guv, a one-nighter, a week, a season on the sands, your face on the telly, the back end of a cow. When they were living down in Poverty Street, nobody knocked at their door, for when you're living down in Poverty Street, folks all know you're poor. But when your bit of silver turns into gold it drives away all care, and then you'll find that everybody's knocking at your door, when you're living in Golden Square.

When Glynis came to London from Ireland, it was in so many ways, in every way she now realises, a different planet. If she was up town, late at night in Leicester Square there was an old woman used to stand about, waiting for the theatres to empty. She wore a headscarf, an old cotton coat with the hem coming down, a few teeth, socks rumbling her ankles, hands raw from whatever she did in the day, the scent of doss house about her. If Glynis was thereabouts she would find her, as if lured by the promise of a nightingale in song. The woman had a voice that altered the night, a voice you could take away deep, far away into the dark, like a gift from somewhere not on a map and never likely to be. You couldn't mistake her because it was always the same headscarf and of course the same voice and very probably the same socks, given away just like the night before or the night before that and tomorrow and so on and stretching back who knew how far? Sometimes, too, if the moon was right and you were lucky, the same song.

All in a day my heart grew sad, misfortune came my way. I had to learn the whole bitter truth, all in a single day. The man that I worshipped as I loved my life, after saying he'd make me his wife, courted another young girl on the sly, so I goes straight up to him. Look, Bill, says I. Bid me goodbye for ever, never come back no more, think of the heart you've gone and broke of the donor you used to adore. Marry the girl you fancy, I wish you luck, I do. But I mean to tarry, 'cos I'll never marry if I can't be tied up to you.

Glynis would stand, whatever the weather, waiting for that song, the heartbreak that cracked through the old woman's voice. All in a day. Glynis would turn back into the crowds before anyone saw the tears start. Looking down from Monty's office window where Poverty Corner had once thronged with the hopeful, she felt them prick again. Where were they, the forgotten ones? Where had they gone, and taken the songs with them? East End, West End, all around the town, the kids play ring-a'rosie, London Bridge is falling down. Boys and girls together, me and Johnny Brown, trip the light fantastic on the streets of London Town.

No good in looking for the old woman. She'd died long ago or festered in a workhouse. It had got into the London newspapers, but none discovered her name, except she'd come from Ireland, as Glynis had, and like Glynis never got the feel or the sense of it off her. In a different time, if Ted Grant had got into hot water, Glynis might have plucked the old woman out of obscurity and whisked her off to Cromer. She doubted the old woman had ever so much as seen the sea, except in Ireland where you couldn't miss it. At the convent, Sister Agathe had more than once expressed regret at not seeing it. 'I was too urban,' she'd tell Glynis, 'before I came to Jesus.'

Glynis reminded herself of that, and someone had once said it to her, remarking that life was for living. It seemed a remarkably straightforward description of what life should be. If Margate was down in Regent Street, Blackpool in Leicester Square. If the Isle of Man was somewhere in the Strand, wouldn't it be grand, listening to the band? If Brighton fair was in Trafalgar Square, Piccadilly all surrounded by the sea, you could bathe with all the boys down Bond Street. Oh, what a grand place London Town would be!

She supposed, later, she'd felt some connection with the old woman's voice and the affair of Cromer Pier. Somewhere between imagination and space the two thoughts fused, the beginning of a possibility. To her surprise, Monty hadn't laughed her out or discounted it, but left it in the hinterland that contained them. He'd taught her the business these last ten years. It was time he let her spread her wings. Let's all go into the ballroom, Glynis thought, the ballroom beside the sea, where the M C calls to the dancers, 'Take your partners, for the Lancers!'. Oh, let's all go into the ballroom and we'll have a rare old spree, where the girls are found tripping it round and round, in the ballroom by the sea!

Since 1950, the BBC had made a television success of *The Good Old Days*, a sort of recreation of music-hall broadcast from Leeds City Varieties. There seemed no reason why Cromer shouldn't have its own version with – Glynis' ace card – two names that would draw them in, one old, one new. Pensioners with a pound in their pocket invaded Cromer in September, so give them a big star, one they'd remember from years back. Then, for the young, an up-and-coming pop-singer, a good-looker.

'Gary Rage,' said Monty, even sounding a little excited, although it hadn't been his idea, but he'd come back into the room having suffered yet another call about a pink toothbrush from Max Bygraves.

'Gary? Would he do it?' asked Glynis. 'Could he?'

'He's only got a personal appearance in Solihull for the opening of a launderette, otherwise he's free those weeks. He was up for a spot on *6.5 Special* next month but it looks as if they're going with Adam Faith.'

'What if they rip up the seats? They did with Tommy Steele.'

'Steele?' Monty puffed his lips out. 'Five minute wonder! They think he's Elvis Presley. He'll be over and done with in a year. These boys are flashes in the pan.'

'They're products. Gary wouldn't have got far, would he, as Harry Catchpole?'

'No, but calling him Gary Rage… Coming it a bit strong, isn't it?'

'Well, there's Marty Wilde, isn't there? You must admit it's an improvement on Reg Patterson. Give them the right name and these lads are up and away.'

'Well, Harry'll do a hell of a sight better than last year's show at Cromer. *Summer Salad*! Why make a show out to be vegetarian? All right, I'll ring him.'

'Fine. And you'd better get used to calling him Gary. But he's only half of the idea, Monty. New and old, remember? That's where your expertise comes in. It's like I said. Where do the people go? Pop songs for the youngsters, music-hall for the oldies. Except it's dead, isn't it?'

'Dead? Who's dead?'

'Dead or dying. Music-hall was never going to last for ever, no more than people like Harry will.'

'The London theatres, they'll survive, but not the music-halls, not the people's palaces you'll find in any town or city worth its name, the Hippodromes, the Empires and Metropoles. Shall I tell you what'll happen? In a couple of years you won't be able to open a local newspaper without reading about them closing down. Films, nude shows, tatty touring revues. A few more years and those old slaphappy entertainments will be gone. A great pity, by the way. I have a great fondness for tat. The music-halls will go, some up in flames. Some will change hands so many times and go through so many rebirths that people won't have an idea in hell as to what's going on inside them. Councils will use any excuse to be rid of them. Rat infestations – no surprise there; there's never been a shortage of rats in this business – or fire hazards, and close them down and sell the land for redevelopment. And when the music-halls go, everything they ever meant goes with it. Saddest thing is, they'll never be replaced. You can't reproduce what's lost. The air's all wrong.'

'I don't know,' said Glynis. 'We may be just in time to find some of the forgotten ones.'

CHAPTER TWO

In the Norfolk village of Branlingham, Mr and Mrs Jones sat still as plaster saints in the front parlour of Red Cherry House. It seemed the best way to sit when a Church of England vicar called, even if this example of a clergyman was almost a friend of the family. Usually, Doris Jones wasted no time in offering a variety of home-baked delicacies helped down by torrents of boiling tea. On this occasion, she remained seated beside her husband, two plaster saints dying for a cuppa.

'You see, vicar,' George Jones began, clearing his throat, 'we don't like to mention it, but there's that other little matter.'

'Ah!' The Revd Challis dropped his head and nodded in appreciation of the inevitable confrontation. 'The other matter. Indeed.'

'If you don't mind us mentioning it, vicar,' said Mrs Jones, her breath short from over-emphatic crimping of the edges of the Bramley apple pie that even now was golden-browning in the oven.

'Not that we believe what they write in the papers,' said Mr Jones, feeling for his pipe. 'Rubbish, most of it, and the rest made up, I dare say, but even so. I mean, *News of the World*...'

'Quite, Mr Jones, quite.' The Revd Challis shrugged his shoulders in an appropriately Christian manner. 'Well, what can I say?'

As it turned out, he said exactly what he said on the other occasions he was challenged about his role in the Episcopal Parsnip Scandal. The case, concerning the inappropriate use of a root vegetable, had rocked the foundations of the diocese, making the front pages of national newspapers. The Revd Challis had indeed been mentioned in connection with the sordid affair, but his Bishop had absolved him of all blame, and the young curate most closely associated with the unsavoury details had been removed to a distant corner of the British Isles. Although the Revd Challis' respectability was proved beyond doubt, he was disappointed to find that after several weeks of St Barnabas at Knee being crammed with coach-parties of strangers, his congregation had all too soon reverted to single numbers.

'Not that we believed it for a second, did we, George?' exclaimed Mrs Jones, beckoning to her husband to shake his head in agreement.

'And so to the matter in hand. I don't think you can have guessed why I've called.'

'Well,' said Mrs Jones, 'I wouldn't be surprised if it wasn't something to do with next year's village festivities. After that last one was such a success and all.'

This was a perfect cue for the Revd Challis to break the tense atmosphere with happy recollection of the recent Branlingham Festival of Arts and Flower Arrangement, in which Doris Jones had played Annie Oakley in his production of *Annie Get Your Gun*. Owing to the last-minute indisposition of Mr Braithwaite from the chemists, the local postmistress Miss Simms had manfully taken over the role of Wild Bill Hickock, with remarkable success.

With not a moment of rehearsal, her expert lassoing had been a sensation, threatening to steal the show from Mrs Jones, for whom a painfully protracted kitchen scene, in which Ado Annie made a Bramley apple pie, had been interpolated.

Owing to the chronic shortage of male choristers, some of the less obviously female ladies of the village had been cast as cowpokes. One member of the audience had complimented local librarian Blodwyn Williams on the effectiveness of her false moustache, only to learn that it was Blodwyn's home-grown. In the circumstances, it seemed only fair that Lord Darting should take the role of a slinky dance-hall girl, and the exposure of his twig-like thighs above fish-net stockings was much appreciated. On opening night, much excitement surrounded the on-stage shoot-outs when, a publicity stunt conceived by the Revd Challis, live ammunition was used. This was not repeated at subsequent performances, the chairwoman of the rural council having informed his reverence that he was financially responsible for repairing the bullet-hole in her municipal hat. When these convivial recollections of theatrical triumphs faded, the Revd Challis warmed to the reason for his visit.

'It's about Francis and Gordon. How would you feel about them having a fortnight's break in Cromer before they return to school after the summer holiday?'

'Oh yes?' said Mr Jones. 'And who's going to afford that? We're not made of money, reverend.'

'Oh, they would be paid, Mr Jones, and free bed and board in a very comfortable lodgings, run by an ex-schoolmaster at St Basil's and his wife, the Brownlows. Mr Brownlow knows the boys well, taught both Francis and Gordon, and has the highest regard for them. It's a fisherman's cottage, almost on the beach. A delightful spot, and all that bracing sea air …'

'What's the catch?' said Mr Jones, getting into his inquisitorial stride and still not convinced about the parsnip.

'I'm not sure there is one,' said the Revd Challis. 'Let me explain. I think to an extent it was I who first introduced Francis and Gordon to the magical world of theatre. You will recall the occasion, I know.'

'Recall it,' cried Mrs Jones. 'I should say I do! You getting the boys into that lovely show at Norwich Hippodrome, and then us finding out the star was no other than my long-lost niece Glenda. Of course, she'd changed her name by then. She were christened Glenda Clatten, you see … doesn't look good in lights. She had to change it to Bunty Rogers.' Mrs Jones said this with a flourish that suggested she understood every fine detail of theatrical life.

'Indeed,' said the reverend. 'That experience, of course, was to involve Francis and Gordon in the case of the Pearl of Thalia. You remember, Mr Jones?'

Mr Jones said he did, although his mind was drifting, remembering Bunty Rogers and the girls in the show, draped around classical ruins with barely a few strips of muslin to protect them from the cool Grecian nights.

'I think we may safely say that that was when the boys "got the bug". That, of course, led on to them being taken on as best boys for that extraordinary film.'

'Oh, yes.' Mr Jones' memory was working overtime. 'That girl wasn't half bad, neither.'

'That's as may be, George,' said Mrs Jones, 'but we don't know what this here break in Cromer would entail.'

The Jones turned expectantly towards their vicar.

'Care,' he replied. 'Care of the elderly.'

CHAPTER THREE

I

On Wednesdays, Perry did the shopping. Turning the corner at the end of Grantchester Street, he looked up to the third floor window of Waldow Mansions. Elsie hadn't moved, not surprising because he'd put the break on the wheelchair before he left. She'd expect him to wave, even though he'd be back in the room before she knew it, so as he turned the corner he put down the heaviest bag and waggled his free hand at her.

She must've dozed off in his absence. Her face had a lopsided way about it when she came to, he could see it even at this distance, forty-five strides to the front door because he always counted them from the junction with Hensgrove Road. He swapped hands for the bags because the heaviest was biting into his fingers, already semi-paralysed. He was disappointed to count forty-nine strides by the time he put the key in the door, wondering where the extra four had come from. Perhaps he was slowing down. Elsie was forever dropping hints about the keep fit sessions for the elderly at the community centre, when the old wore shorts.

'Did you get everything?'

He'd marked off the list. Once out of the flat, his mind went to other things, so the list was essential if he wasn't to forget.

'What took you so long?' asked Elsie.

The usual, he told her, his back turned. The crowds in the shops, a mix-up at the till, a surly girl at a bus stop enquiring if he had any loose change, the search for a particular product of which the store manager had said he had no knowledge. Nevertheless the staff initiated a thorough investigation of the shelves and storeroom, with no success. After, he bumped into a colleague from the shoe shop where he'd worked part-time, and stopped to direct an old lady to the local library. Thinking he'd left his purse at the newspaper shop, he walked all the way back to rescue it, only to discover it had been in his pocket all the time.

It had been a time-consuming morning. Unhappy with the look of tomatoes in the greengrocer on Bartlett Road, it had taken him ten minutes to walk to the supermarket where the tomatoes at least looked the right degree of red. All this activity must have accounted for an hour or more, but just in case that wasn't convincing he said there'd been a contretemps at the crossroads where an old man, not much older than himself, had collapsed, attracting passers-by who considered whether mouth to mouth resuscitation should be attempted on someone with false teeth for fear of them being dislodged. Elsie perked up at this. From the window of the flat she could make out some of the roundabout at the end of Warwick Street and even a little bit of the crossroads but she'd seen nothing of the commotion Perry described. Perhaps there'd be something in the papers later. The news in Sunderland was usually depressing.

'Swiss rolls,' said Perry, unpacking his bags as if he were a conjuror producing rabbits, 'white bread, chocolate log, Madeira cake, crumpets … All aboard for the Constipation Express.'

'You are a dear, Perry. My auntie had a sweet tooth, runs in the family.'

'Your auntie had *no* teeth. I'll put the kettle on.'

'It'll suit you!' Elsie crackled, her rusty laugh ringing through the flat. It had been her idea to incorporate jokes into the act.

Today, he had taken his usual route, before the shopping bags became cumbersome, at first stopping off at St Godric's. Only a couple of streets further and there was St Agnes, busy even at this time of the morning, one or two people with bowed heads, but nothing doing because it was still daylight. St John's had a celestial silence that frightened him for a moment, and a cistern was overflowing. It was almost a relief to get back into the street. From here it was only the matter of turning a corner to St Peter's. He recognised one of the men there, and looked away just in time. He'd already used up a fair bit of shopping time. Imagining Elsie's 'What took you so long?', he put on speed and made his first purchase of the morning.

'Come back and we'll get cosy' she called into the kitchen, the fire in her belly young again, and palmy. 'Monty Desmond still wants us! Imagine! Monty Desmond!'

Perry made the tea, keeping quiet, checking his face in the mirror, different angles, waiting for the inevitable boiling of the kettle. Elsie would be wanting to persuade him about having new photos done. The public would expect it, she said, they couldn't be fobbed off with the ones they'd had done forty-odd years ago. His left side was best. He'd always started like that, presenting his profile to the audience soon as the curtain went up. His left side was more manly, no doubt of it, but of course when Elsie started up with 'Only A Rose' he had to move eventually, full face, into the light, as she'd need shifting.

It owned him, that light, warmed him through and through, brought him into a semblance of life. What he couldn't do was look into her eyes. He knew what it was. On stage, it was as if he belonged to her, as if they were everything to one another, that they existed alone in an idyll of unending ecstasy. It repulsed him, but his inability to disappoint or hurt her kept him pinned as if he were a captured butterfly.

It hardly mattered that they'd never married, or that they had been engaged since 1939. People, in the street, in the theatres, assumed they were husband and wife. The illusion worked for them, if not for Perry handing Elsie downstage in earlier days from the podium on which she had been discovered standing by an overflowing floral arrangement in an ornamental pot, her crinolines bouncing about her buttocks as she descended, Perry wondering by what route, even if he were interested, he would access such a garment for sexual gratification.

'Do you know, Perry, I think it's going to work. I'm ready for it. I think it's the right time.'

He put down the tea tray, his legs heavy under him.

'Elsie, you can't move. How would it work?'

'We tweak it. Change the bill matter for starters. I've been thinking "Immobile Duettists".'

'You may not have noticed, but I'm not immobile,' said Perry. 'I move about.'

'You can do bloody cartwheels so far as I'm concerned. Well, of course the moving movements will all be down to you, but, funny how things turn about, I think it'll give the act a twist, something novel. I thought we might start with me on a sort of throne, encrusted with roses, like a swing that's been grounded. I mean, I can still use my arms, and eyes, always got them going with my eyes. You don't lose those skills. Not when you're an artiste. And you keep changing position so they can see a bit of movement moving about if they want.'

'Elsie, it was forty years ago.'

'I know, Perry. It's magic, all over again.'

'It won't work. It's all in the past. It won't come back.'

'But it has, Perry. You and me, Grenville and Elsie. It may be the one last wonderful thing to happen to either of us.'

Perry pours the tea, trying to remember it's left that's his best side. Elsie is humming 'Only A Rose', lifting a tea cup and practising her arms.

II

The inspectors had gone by tea-time, so Deirdre Corbett put her feet up in the office. It had been a different pair to the last time, a balding man with a clipboard and lisp and a younger woman with hennaed hair and a poncho, poking about the place, picking up tubes of ointment, opening cupboards, running their fingers over skirting boards and stooping to speak to the inmates. Not that they'd have got any sense out of them. Deirdre noticed the girl with red hair going into Room 22, so it was just as well she'd sneaked a couple of sleeping tablets into the occupant's cornflakes that morning. Old Mother McPhee would have had plenty to say, but she was out for the count. The girl with the artificially-coloured hairdo had bumped into Deirdre on her way back into the corridor and said 'Bless her cotton socks', presumably a reference to Mother McPhee, so

Deirdre had given one of her synthetic smiles, an imitation of that used by Mother Teresa. As if they could afford cotton socks! Running the place was more a charity than a business. The sign at the entrance read 'Evermore: Rest for the Weary', but that didn't include the staff.

The television was on loud enough to cut out the alarm bells that provided a continuous soundtrack. Deirdre poured a little too much gin into the tonic, settling in for the quiz programme about to start. It was the one with that handsome host in tight trousers, the material clearly under strain as he floated around the studio. There were the accounts to do because it was the end of the month, and they were low on toiletries. She'd get them from the market stall tomorrow, the one that specialised in fire sales. Naturally, there was a mark-up when the monthly accounts went out to relatives. Corkage, she called it. There'd be plenty of time to falsify the amounts after she'd watched the programme, which turned out to be disappointing because now the boy's trousers billowed around his thighs. A trailer for a documentary programme followed. The BBC had sent an undercover reporter into a care home in Shropshire. An old woman was crying out, but you couldn't hear what she was saying. It was one of the many problems associated with care of the elderly that people didn't appreciate.

Deirdre kicked off her heels and helped herself to a Caramel Delight from the Milk Tray box. She'd taken it off Room 53, having diagnosed its occupant as lactose intolerant. She was just pushing it through her lipsticked lips when she heard the latch at the front gate go. Not bothering to get up, she twisted her head to see who it was. For a moment, she fancied she caught a glimpse of two figures, struggled to her stockinged feet and moved to an angle of the room, half concealed beside a window. It was only Mother McPhee's visitor, that dumpy little woman who came regular as anything every other day, hardly a squeak escaping from her, so unobtrusive that she barely mattered. Deirdre hadn't heard or seen her come in. She was no threat, anyway; always smiled back if Deirdre happened to see her, never a hint of a complaint. Looked like Old Mother McPhee too.

Like all visitors, the woman had been informed that the door of 'Evermore' was permanently locked, purely for the safety of residents. Did they want their elderly loved ones roaming the streets at any time of the day or night in their pyjamas? If they looked doubtful about this policy, Deirdre began speaking of hypothermia, of traffic collisions, unattended railway crossings, and drownings should the inmates make the fifteen miles to the nearest river. That shut them up. Furthermore, it would be helpful if they could telephone for an appointment before visiting. With the dumpy little woman, it had been easier to allow her open access.

The sound of a car engine sent Deirdre back to the window. The rump of a taxi, its engine running, was clearly visible now. The dumpy woman was clambering into the back. Deirdre shifted her body this way and that for a better view. At this angle, it was difficult to see what was happening, and for a moment it looked as if there might be two people in the taxi. The driver, having got out of the taxi to help Mrs McPhee's visitor into the vehicle, was blocking the view. The door slammed shut, and the taxi drove off.

The television sound wasn't loud enough to drown out the volume of buzzing set off by the number of alarms rung in the rooms of the distressed. It had been a frustrating day. To crown it all Deirdre had to fork out £20 to the woman who always alerted her when the council would be arriving for a surprise inspection. Still, it was a price worth paying. Remembering that there was no rest for the matron of a well-drilled care home for the weary, Deirdre sank back into her armchair, turned up the volume and helped herself to a Raspberry Creme. She could only hope for tighter trousers next week. Five minutes later, an assistant put her head round the door and told her Mrs McPhee's room was empty. What was more, she wasn't on the premises, and those old photographs in silver frames she had on the table by her bed had gone too.

CHAPTER FOUR

I

'And this,' said Lady Darting, nodding towards the room she had just revealed to her guest as if it were a prized relic in the British Museum, 'is the Pink Room.'

'I should say it's more of a mauve.'

Lady Darting knew better. It had been the Purple Room until the sun had sucked the colour out of it.

'Marshall and Snelgrove will bring up your luggage. The Eastern Electricity Board will bring a tray of tea.'

Her ladyship, who seldom did anything as commonplace as leaving a room, withdrew sinuously, leaving the stranger to wonder at the great British institutions that would at any moment be arriving, unaware that Lord and Lady Darting, confused by the changes in servant personnel, called them after the companies at which they had previously been employed.

Hattie Prince stood, her back to the door, taking in the diminished splendour, the family portraits, some mere daubs, that dotted the walls, seemingly peering down at her as if making up their minds as to her suitability, the heavily brocaded curtains that smelled of must, the distinguished and ancient rugs, worn, inviting the old to trip and become terminally hospitalised. The glass of the great window that looked down on what had once been the creation of an unmarried Victorian lady gardener was encrusted with grime, making the plants seem to be waving in a fog, but no doubt Lady Darting's handyman – probably the British Broadcasting Corporation – was at this very moment mounting a ladder to rectify the view. Yes, thought Hattie, looking around and beginning to feel the space, this would do nicely.

She should never have gone into that nursing home. 'Evermore', indeed! It had been a Monday morning, ten o'clock, when the neighbour called through the door, thirty-six hours after Hattie's legs had gone awol. The doctor fished the key on string that was posted through the letterbox and tried to move her about. It wasn't a hospital case, he said, and that came as a relief, her thinking of the way she'd strutted about and pranced and posed all those years. It was a case of respite care, he said. A change of scene, that's how he put it, and by then Enid had learned of her indisposition and caught the tube from Pimlico. The doctor recommended the 'Evermore', having known the matron, although he didn't say how. It was accessible from Pimlico and from Hattie's council flat at the back of the Coliseum. Handy was the word he used.

'You'll soon pick up and be back at full strength, Mrs McPhee' he said, without much conviction.

Hattie knew better. There'd been talk of a late summer engagement, and she hadn't worked since Eastbourne Hippodrome. She stroked the veins in her legs, switching her head about to get an all-round look at the problems. She agreed to the 'Evermore' because there seemed to be no choice, and as it turned out it was probably a good move because the moment she arrived she made up her mind to get out as soon as her legs would let her. Enid came every other day. The matron took no notice, never so much as offered Enid a cup of tea or asked how her journey on the tube had been, or what her relationship to Old Mother McPhee might be. Matron had briefly wondered about her latest resident's past. There were all those old photographs on her bedside table, a sailor, a guardsman, a smart man about town, vaguely Edwardian and foxed.

And on the Thursday, it was obvious that Enid knew something and wouldn't say. Hattie knew as soon as her sister walked into the room.

'You've heard from Monty Desmond?'

'Sorry, dear?'

'You've heard from Monty, haven't you?'

Since they were children, Hattie had always known everything going on in Enid's mind. It came naturally when you were an elder sister.

'I don't know,' said Enid. 'I really don't know what to think.'

'Well, you tell me what you think and I'll tell you what I know.'

'He's made an offer. Better than you had at Eastbourne. But it's too soon, Hattie. You're not fit enough. Three days rehearsal and a fortnight's run, two matinees a week ...'

'Oh, I love matinees! It's when it all seems completely unreal. When do we start?'

'You shouldn't do it, love, really you mustn't.'

'And what about the billing? What did he say?'

'He agreed. Top of the bill.'

'So, when do we start? There'll be the digs to arrange.'

'He said that was all taken care of, we hadn't to worry. You'll be at a lovely old Hall, just you, a guest of the owners. Aristocracy.'

Enid knew all was lost, that she had just handed Hattie the icing on the cake.

'Why are you looking at your watch, love?' asked Hattie. 'Am I keeping you?'

'No. It's … the taxi. I've got the taxi waiting.'

It was the confession Enid knew she would have to make. Hattie winked at her.

'There's that blue travel bag in the cupboard, love. You can scoop everything in there.'

Keeping quiet as a mouse was no difficulty for Enid. Eighty years on, she was as happy now as she had always been to do Hattie's bidding, but it surprised her that she felt so little nervousness about helping her sister escape. She'd cased the joint earlier in the week, working out how to cross the space between Hattie's bedroom and the front door to freedom, and none of the hinges squeaked, and the hedge that ran along the frontage of 'Evermore' would hide them, except for the few seconds it took to clear the exit and reach the gate as they made their way to the getaway car.

Hattie manoeuvred her legs out of bed, flexing each as if making sure she could make it out to the pavement. With bowed heads and shuffled breath, she and Enid moved as noiselessly as Cold War spies. For Moira McPhee, alias Hattie Prince, 'England's Premier Male Impersonator', another adventure had begun.

II

The shoreline and pier at Cromer has long been overshadowed by the imposing hotel looming above its handsome promenade. At the end of the eighteenth century, Pierre le Francoise, a refugee from the French Revolution, acquired the land from Lord Suffield, opening his hostelry in 1830, when William IV was on the throne of England. Six years on, it was officially declared a boarding-house. Some thought it a 'bawdy' house, ramshackle and indecent, until in 1845 it was renamed the Hotel de Paris, suddenly continental and unexpectedly respectable. The development of the railways, a boost to tourism, was as much a curse as a blessing to the de Paris as it increasingly faced competition from other hotels such as the Grand and the Cliftonville, quick to take advantage of the holidaying traffic. Some prospered and some failed (the Grand proved less grand than it sounded and was demolished) but through it all the de Paris held fast, face lifted in 1891 when local architect George Skipper designed a new building to stand where le Francoise had long ago opened his business.

Now, at the fag end of a damp, bedraggled summer, the de Paris gave off no hint of French excess. More than once, holidaymakers dragging up the winding path from the lower promenade looked up at its towering presence, imagining the prices of its rooms. The building, as buildings are inclined to, took no notice of this, always having kept itself to itself, confident of its faintly Gallic splendour, its slightly forbidding facade at once suggesting that unimaginably luxurious delights awaited within, delights unavailable to the *hoi polloi*.

Today, the curved forecourt of the hotel was crammed with people, others having staked a claim on the upward paths to get the best view they could. Some had travelled miles for the occasion, timed in the local newspaper for two o'clock. A No-Parking sign had been put out for the expected limousine, rumoured to be big, and American, and open-top. This, of course, would only be possible if the day stayed dry, but, unusually for early September,

43

the sun was having a baking day. The ice cream kiosk at the top of the prom was doing a brisk business, and the entrance to the hotel had been flung open so that music played within washed out into the streets. It was 'You Are Not The Girl', and Gary Rage, who would shortly be arriving in the big American and hopefully open-top car, was singing it on a gramophone record. One of the girls in the crowd who knew such things said it was number thirty in the charts, and going up.

Below, at the entrance to the pier, Monty Desmond wasn't so sure. There was a lot riding on this show, *Forget-Me-Not* (he and Glynis had worried for days about the title). He couldn't afford another disaster after Herne Bay. You'd expect audiences to flock when the rain was pissing down day after day, but it had kept them away. After the eight week season at the Cosy Den he'd only just recouped the production costs. At Herne Bay, of course, he hadn't had a big name. Now, he had two. Glynis had argued about the posters, as per, and he'd had Gary Rage's agent and Hattie battling with him to get their names top of one another. He stood and looked at the finished article, standing a little too long because two holidaymakers, the woman in a swimsuit and the man in rolled up trouser legs and a vest, stood by his side and gave the poster the once-over.

'Ooh,' said the woman. 'Gary Rage. Seen him on the telly. Who's the other one?'

'Hattie Prince.'

'Who's she when she's at home?'

'Never heard of her. Mind yourself, Doreen. That ice cream's dripping.'

There'd been a philosophy about Monty when he'd decided on his topliners. Hattie Prince, star of the Edwardian music-hall, to please the oldies, the pensioners who strolled up and down the pier and took tea in dark corners of the dwarfed tearooms of the town, and Gary Rage, sexually alluring if he was your sort of person, up-to-date, for the younger generation. 'Hip' probably covered both categories: genuine hip for the young, artificial hip for the old. If Rage had got a record contract with Decca rather than Pye, there would have been no argument, he'd have been top of the bill. As it was, the boy had only been in the business a few weeks, striking it lucky with Hughie Green on *Opportunity Knocks* and getting a spot a couple of weeks ago on the BBC's *6.5 Special*. Gary Rage might turn out to be a gold-mine. It was a risk, and one that Monty could back away from if need be. Hattie Prince, meanwhile: she was a different story. She'd endured. My God, how she'd endured! 86 and still enduring!

When Monty looked up to the hotel, Glynis was there, standing at the promontory, waving at him and pointing at her watch. The wonder boy must be about to arrive. The cheering began as Monty started up the slopes, squeezing through the crowds to get even a glance of the event he'd organised. He could hear the anarchic roar of the big American open-top car as it wound into view, its vulgar zooming soon drowned by the yelping that poured from the on-lookers.

Those who had seen Gary Rage on the television were not disappointed. The studio cameras had completely failed to relay the brilliant freshness of his complexion, the luxurious curve of his lips, the remotely vague look in his eyes. As the jubilation around him rose again, he clambered onto the back seat of the Cadillac, a blond Adonis rising clear above the waves of Cromer, something rare and divine, as if a god had come around the corner to stay, if only for a span.

III

'Welcome, Mr Rage. Welcome to the Hotel de Paris!'

The words were English, but Monsieur Raymond, general manager of the hotel and the crimping genius of its hairdressing salon, spoke with a French accent, although he came from West Runton. What a coup it would be if this guest could be persuaded to visit the salon. What he could do with that blond quiff!

'I trust you had a good journey.'

'We're fine, thank you,' said Glynis, used to being her client's ears and voice. 'Mr Rage has had a tiring journey. If he could be shown to his room.'

'Of course, but it is not a *room*. For so special a guest, what else but the Henry Blogg Suite.'

'We booked a room.'

'At no extra cost to yourselves, of course.'

'Blogg?' said Rage. The voice came softly, music in a tunnel.

'Named after one of Cromer's finest heroes. I'm sure you will be very comfortable there.'

Raymond clicked his fingers. Bags were snatched up and taken to the lift. As Gary Rage turned to follow them, he was aware that the staff had been lined up as if for a royal presentation. He smiled at them, said 'Hello everyone' and moved on.

Betty Moore had worked at the hotel for years. 'Well,' she said, 'I wouldn't mind bumping into him under the pier after dark.'

IV

Greenbanks, up beyond the edge of the cliffs, was modesty itself compared to the Hotel de Paris. Mrs Freebody was its widowed landlady, taking in theatricals, which, in a sleepy seaside place such as Cromer, was a seasonal business. Having just waved off six members of the profession from the long-running summer show on the pier (a female singer, a conjuror, an Indian rope-dancer, the gin-soaked musical director, a trick cyclist and a Hungarian who kept seals in a bath) she had been delighted to extend her own season by welcoming in some of the *Forget-Me-Not* company. They would be bedding in today, and begin work at the theatre tomorrow.

The first to arrive were the conjurors, an older man and his on-stage assistant, registering with Mrs Freebody as the twin beds. She took them up to the third floor back. Next to arrive was a woman with hair that had had a whole bottle of something coloured poured over it. She smelled slightly of sweat and peppermint, a Miss Driscoll, but she had nice manners although her hands trembled, and seemed quite content with the parched backside of a room on the ground floor. After lunch, a taxi drew up, out of which stepped a man of average height, average looks and little discernible character. This was Heron Makepeace, who was no sooner installed in the little sitting-room at the front on the second floor than he began vocal exercises, pulling in his paunch as he did so.

The next to ring Mrs Freebody's doorbell was more of a problem. He called himself Parliamentary Pete, standing on her threshold with his wife, who made it clear that she was not staying but would come back to collect him when the two-week engagement was over. Mrs Freebody had smartened up the second floor box-room (the man with the seals, or the seals, had left it in a disgusting state) especially for him, only to learn that Mr Pete (she could think of nothing else to call him) had recently lost a leg, and could on no account be expected to put pressure on the remaining one (or the other one, if involved) to climb flights of steps. A discreet word with Miss Driscoll resolved the situation, she agreeing to take the second-floor box-room, so that Mr Pete's left leg (i.e. the one that was left) was not overworked. Mrs Freebody noticed that Miss Driscoll smelled even more strongly of peppermint than earlier, and their conversation had started the tremor in her hands.

Mrs Freebody had been warned about her final guests. Receiving the list of arrivals from Glynis, memory nudged as she read 'Grenville and Elsie'. Of course! Peregrine Grenville (wasn't it? – Perry to his intimates) and Elsie Balls, soprano. A sort of Anne Ziegler and Webster Booth act, singing songs that grandma used to sing before anyone could stop her. Glynis had intimated that life had not been kind to them in recent years, Peregrine having not worked professionally for the last twenty and that Miss Balls was confined to a wheelchair. Mrs Freebody, keen as mustard, had directed Glynis to the ramp at the approach to Greenbanks' front door. The seals had found it especially useful. By four o'clock that afternoon, all Mrs Freebody's guests from the *Forget-Me-Not* company had booked in. There would be a celebratory tea party in her front room at five.

CHAPTER FIVE

I

'You'll get nowhere but where you're bound, lad.'

Len waited. It'd take a while for that one to sink in. That grizzle-haired stick of a man was prone to such unfathomable statements. Henry was old enough to be Len's grandfather. Come to think of it, that might not have been a bad thing. It made him more northern, too, that unexpected benevolence pouring out of him like he was Wilfred Pickles turning on the charm at a sardine canning factory. Uncanny, because Wilfred was on the wireless in the background, as it happened at a canning factory. It didn't seem quite right, Len being with Henry in Brighton. The north was a world away. The wireless crackled hysterically as the factory exploded with a sense of uniqueness, of belonging to itself and to everyone inside it, as though holding its sides it would withstand everything that life might throw at it. Henry turned it off.

'Not if you go on as you are, any rate.'

There'd been such an unearthly silence since his previous words, except for *Have a Go!* on the wireless, that Len had trouble connecting them. Nothing to get worked up about.

Any time soon the old man would start up about footwear. He didn't have to wait long.

'Look to your boot straps, lad. Them's what'll pull you up. There's them as has to do nowt to get on in t'world and them as has the knack of never having a clue. Of course, that's a knack that's no use to anyone, when the whole point of knacks is for them to be there when you need one. You've proved yourself here, after all.'

Had he? Len wasn't so sure. He'd only walked the streets for Henry those few weeks last summer, advertising Henry's guest house ('Rooms of Comfort. A place to rest the weary head. Considerate rates for the Homeless'). How did that count?

'Hey up. I was your sandwich board man. I walked up and down every street in Brighton. It's an unskilled occupation. What did that prove?'

'Proved you can carry a weight on your back, lad. Just as well to get that off your chest. You'll not want to say you haven't got that over and done with in later life. Proves you can weather a storm.'

'I nipped under bus shelters if it as much as drizzled.'

'Proves you don't mind looking like a balm pot.'

'Did I?'

'You never saw what the sandwich board had printed at the back.'

'Right.'

Len looked out to where the sea should have been, but it was out.

'So, where does that leave me?'

'Know what I'd do, lad? If I were your age.'

'Twenty-three.'

'I'd take a stare at meself in the mirror.'

'Would that help?'

'Probably not. The fairy that gave out good looks must have been distracted at your moment of birth.'

'I'm not much of a looker,' said Len. 'It's one of the few things that's never worried me. They don't want looks, they want qualifications. What have you done? That's what they want to know. What've you done, where have you come from, and where's your accent and the bit of paper to prove it?'

'Fuck that. Smoke and mirrors. You'll not be wanting that if you've the sense you were born with.'

It was Henry's turn to look out to sea. He came to much the same conclusion as his ex-sandwich-board man: the sea would always be there, even when out.

'Where are you working now?'

'New Clarendon.'

Henry bristled. It didn't take much for him to recall an unfortunate encounter with the New Clarendon's idea of a prawn cocktail. He'd drawn himself up to his full height, swearing never to darken its portico again, and asked for the chef. The New Clarendon had opened a hundred years ago but even then there'd been nothing new to write home about. Henry's nostrils twitched at the memories. The carpets reeked of Victorian dust and old people's pee, the result of its mid-week half-price-for-pensioners policy.

'Pot washing,' said Len.

'It's a phase. You can rule out mining or bricklaying. You're too fine a lad for such. Not with them fingers.'

'Steady on. Anyone'd think you were after me body.'

Henry took another peep at the sea. His beard had brilliant darts in it when the light slanted across his face.

'Time was.'

His eyes lifted under hooded lids. He'd liked Len from the first, that day he sat next to him at a do in the town hall, liked the way his eyes made a beeline for his, the curve of his knee, touching his own if he shifted his leg, hearing the soft expiration of the lad's breath. He'd looked at Len's face for, what?, no more than five minutes total, and couldn't get his face out of his mind, forcing himself every so often to bring back its features. He'd loved Len ever since, really, depending on what you thought love was.

How had Len not noticed? Heaven knows, the bed was big enough, a grounded gondola dominating the scruffy rag-pile room, waiting to glide through the canals of physical pleasure or sleep, dressed by a counterpane of faded silk roses. Beneath, once-crystal-white sheets of good linen bought in a sale long before the war and now slate grey, long-retired-from-circulation sheets protruding at the fountainhead, once white, now even greyer than stone. There was so much else to look at beside. Best not to dwell on what state the linen in the guests' rooms was in. Not that it mattered. It wasn't a priority for the dispossessed, the refugees from the world's assorted wickedness, the reckless who'd up and walked away from their ramshackle lives, anxious to get their heads down after negotiating Henry's special rate (nothing to pay for the first week and then let's see). Not priorities for the forgotten.

The house in Brighton had long ago decided on a cathedral-like peacefulness. The pedestal sink, the encrusted cupboards of knotted pine or plywood, a wooden table with one severely burned leg, the others perhaps saved by an obliging Fire Brigade, two armchairs lopped out of shape with squelchy welcoming noises, a parrot's cage (empty), a wind-up gramophone, strapped trunks back from some foreign clime or bottom of the bill theatre and never touched since, weather-beaten, time-wearied, tempest-tossed, locked. The spaces left available were dotted with boxes of all shapes and sizes, stacked almost to the ceiling. A few had 'Heinz 57 Varieties' stamped on them, others pretended to be more official, as if this were a place where you discovered reliable information or classified documents. Then, there was the biggest box of all, the one that wasn't made of cardboard.

This was ebony. It must have stood well over six feet. It had double-opening doors at the front, decorated with dragons that had been lacquered some time before the Great War. One time, Len had sneaked open one of the doors when Henry was out of the room. He'd caught a glimpse of thick red velvet curtains lashed with gold, a scent of velvet mustiness and the fog of long-dead heat smouldering within, before he heard Henry's returning footsteps. He wondered on what he was closing the doors. Even now, the longer he looked at the box, he could have sworn the dragons were ready at any moment to writhe into life, their fiery snouts lifting in salute.

'It were me dad's,' said Henry.

'What?'

'That cabinet was me dad's. He were younger than me.'

'That's clever.'

'When he died. On the Somme.'

'Oh, God.'

The sea came in handy when conversation stalled, filling up the gaps between them, even if, still technically out, it could make itself heard. Aware of being ignored for too long, it was working up little volleys of wave and setting them towards the shore. It sounded through the house, Henry's tumbledown not quite on the beach and therefore by no means completely disreputable. The place must have had cracks in it where mice and touring insects and sounds and smells could get in, so the sea had sent in its inevitable rumble.

II

As it happened, the sea had been the soundtrack of his childhood for ten-year-old Len, destined for sandwich-boarding and pot-washing at the not-so-new-if-you-knew-the-facts New Clarendon, taken out of Manchester to a bungalow at the deadest end of Blackpool, Rossall Beach. For two years, the sky had been his roof, driftwood, periwinkles and sea wrack drying under a must-try-harder October sun in a landscape so dominant that it promised to cancel everything that had been before.

His long pointless days on the shore only ended when the woman acting as his mother fetched him in for tea. 'Tea,' she'd call, as if there could be any other reason she might want him back, and then as if he'd been hired out by the hour 'Come in, Leonard Foster.'

That was another of Fate's tricks, having another boy called Leonard (Leonard Spruce) living next door, and Mrs Grantley, not wanting to cause confusion and not willing to call the next-door Leonard in for tea when it was bother enough having to provide it for the other Leonard she'd signed up to. 'Leonard Foster', his pretend mother called, broadcasting it across the shoreline as if he was a boat whose time was up, or a stranger, which of course was how he'd arrived at Mr and Mrs Grantleys and how he'd leave. Didn't she know he'd recognise her voice, no matter how loudly the sea carried on at his side? Even herded animals, separated by foraging, recognised the calls of lowing parents without having to be given full particulars, but this was just another way in which fostered Leonard Foster was set apart.

The worst of it was that Leonard-next-door's mother never called her son by name, only standing square to the sea before shouting 'Where are you, luv?'. It was the more painful because when Leonard Spruce's mother called out to her son, the lilt in her voice was threaded with concern that one day her son (and of course she was his real mother) might no longer be there, running back from the edge of the waves. He'd be gone away, all that childhood happiness stored up in him to make him the braver, the more able to stand it, and then he'd grow old and then he'd die. Her voice had the shadows about it, the knowing that one day his boyhood would end and be taken away from him and his mother and God knew what would happen to them both.

There was no incipient sadness in Mrs Grantley's plea for Leonard Foster's return, but what could he expect? A boy who had come into the Grantley's life through an arrangement that he knew wouldn't last. Mrs Grantley got pregnant with the child she'd told the social she couldn't have just before she signed a form to take charge of Leonard, and he had formed a queue behind the pampered newcomer. A second lucky strike ('Leonard, say hello to your new sister') told him it was only a matter of time before he was packed off back to the Home they'd taken him from.

'Well, Leonard.'

The superintendent at Collingworth House had put his arm around the boy's shoulders, three years older than when he'd left, then shook his hand. Uncle David, they called him, not that it fooled the kids. Len supposed it was a right of passage, the recognition that soon, if not already, he would be a man. Thirteen-year-old Leonard Foster, once fostered, now returned to somewhere called home but with a capital H that somehow made the difference.

When he'd run away was when he met Henry. Fifteen, he'd been, when Henry had said he'd better bring his stuff into the guest house and he'd looked at him as if to say what stuff. Anyway, he'd taken himself in, stuff or no, and never left. It was only now, with the cracks in the plaster flaking, the dust cheese-slice-thick on the sticks of furniture, each suggesting they'd been washed up from a sea-wreck, that he saw Henry as he'd never seen him before. Oh, this was an old man, still with the kindnesses about him, but old, the breath short inside. Len needed to break away, got the job at the New Clarendon, and saw Henry on a visit now and then. And now, with Wilfred Pickles turned off so they could distinguish the sea's murmuring, Henry said he'd had a call. A telephone call from London.

'What about?' asked Len.

'The box,' said Henry.

If Henry hadn't stared at it so hard Len wouldn't have known which box he meant. It was the one with dragons on it, the ebony one that reeked of a secret past, vaguely oriental but just stood there, six feet tall and counting and the dragons at sentry-go.

'Step inside,' said Henry.

Len had never seen him so lithe, never heard him so commanding. All his limbs looked as if they were working together for the first time in a long time. It was only polite to comply. After all the old man had ever done for him, all the times he'd stood by, never questioning, it was the right thing to do to stand up and walk over and step into that box. Once he was inside, Henry pulled at the red plush curtains and closed the front of the box. It must have been on a sort of pivot, because in the dark he could tell the thing was going round and round and Henry was making odd sounds, hissing as if an orchestra was playing mystical music. When it stopped revolving, Henry said 'And now, to open the box.'

Of course, Len didn't know what was happening, being inside and apart, but Henry had opened the door of the box by which Len had gone in.

And Len wasn't there.

CHAPTER SIX

I

'Thing is,' said May. 'You've only got the one.'
　　'You what? What are you talking about? One what? You'll not be able to stay after eight, you know. They turn the visitors out pronto. You'll not be dallying.'

May hadn't supposed they'd be very hospitable, odd when it was a hospital and the two words didn't go together.

'Leg,' she said, clutching her handkerchief because she'd no option but to break the news to him. The staff hadn't the gumption.

'You've only got the one, now.'

Not wanting to see the expression on his face when he looked down the bed, she turned her head, across the ward to where another old man was waiting for something surgical.

'Christ. Christ. What have they done to me, May?'

'The official word is amputation.'

'Well, I'm damned. I could have sworn that foot was itching.'

'They said as much,' said May, hoping to introduce a lighter tone. 'That can be quite normal in the circumstances. And you've still got the other one. Have some more squash.'

'Christ. Of all the times. Christ.'

'I know, Pete. But I don't think it matters.'

'Doesn't matter? Doesn't matter? What the hell do you mean, it doesn't matter?'

'Because I spoke to Monty last night on the blower and he said not to worry. You're expected to make a full recovery, and he still wants you.'

'He does?'

'Well, don't sound so surprised. Have you ever known Monty to go back on his word?'

'No. I mean, he's a funny bugger, we know, but no, if he says it'll be all right.'

'There's time enough, you see. I spoke to the doctor, the one with the stoop and the dirty fingernails. He says you'll be up and about in no time, no stopping you. Anyway, Monty asked me to check the billing.'

'Does he know I've lost the leg?'

'I told him it had to come off.'

'Well, does he think that'll affect the billing?'

'I shouldn't think so, Pete.'

'What's the fuss about, then? It'll be the same as it has been for the last fifty years. Parliamentary Pete; Passes Every Bill.'

II

Mondays, Dorothy goes down the loke to see her mother. Not her real one, but the one who got married to her father. Not that he was her real father, really, not really hers, having been brought into the picture around 1923 long after the one who'd played the original role had retired from the scene. In the evenings on Mondays she watches the television, sitting with Mrs MacNiece in the front room of Twelve Trees at Mayfield Avenue in North Finchley, even though so far as she can make out there are only eleven of them and two of them are really big bushes. She and Mrs MacNiece watch the nine o'clock dramas on independent television. Dorothy makes appropriate comments about the acting and the dialogue when the advertisements come on, and of course Mrs MacNiece, who makes vague allusions to a distant cousin called Louis who is possibly speaking on the Third Programme at that very moment, takes notice of what she says because Dorothy was a theatrical and knows her stuff.

For a change, on Tuesdays Dorothy goes to the park in the summer, takes a coffee and a scone in the mornings at the little café under the sign that says 'The toilets are inspected at regular intervals', although there's never anyone comes near or by in an official capacity whenever she's been there, then in the afternoons her Tuesday walk by the river, scattering any yesterday bread that Mrs MacNiece, much given to cheese on toast, has no further use for. When she walks back to the same spot, like as not the bread's still there. The evenings are much the same on Tuesdays as they are on Mondays, going downstairs and settling into the armchair just in time for the nine o'clock kick off on the telly, and so it is on every night except Sundays when she puts the fire on in her room (one bar) even in the summer because the sun doesn't get into the back room and she's thankful for a cardigan. The Sunday nine o'clock slot on the telly remains a mystery to her, Mrs MacNiece in some faint way having intimated that the holy day removed the need for televisual entertainment, when the set is not switched on, and not mentioned.

Then there's Wednesdays. Dorothy shops, or, more accurately, walks past them, strolls among them, makes knowing nods toward their windows, criticising the merchandise out loud in the streets, and in the afternoons there's sometimes a matinee at the local cinema or a musical show, sometimes even a tour of one she's been in, although nowadays they've got out of the habit of doing *The Maid of the Mountains.*

Thursdays she has father for the day, fetching him on the bus from the Old Folks' Home (council-run) and bringing him back to Twelve Trees where she concocts a sort of lunch for him, the kitchen kindly vacated for the occasion by Mrs MacNiece, her only stipulation that no fish shall be cooked during Dorothy's occupation, so she puts a window on the latch just to make sure. In the afternoons of a Thursday they sit in her upstairs room, although Mrs MacNiece has been known to vacate the sitting room to give them more breathing space. They listen to the clock on the mantelpiece, the late Mr MacNiece's reward after fifty years at the Gas, glancing through magazines in a vague attempt at sophistication, until eight o'clock when she takes him back to the Old Folks' Home, already in darkness, by bus.

Fridays come as a relief. She makes a point of never mapping out her Fridays in advance (always regarded by her since childhood as a day apart, when Catholics prefer to eat fish, although she only likes haddock), looking about her in carefree mode and deciding there and then what the day will bring, week by week.

Saturday is unavoidable and has to be got through. She has always thought it a common day, with a sort of pretend Bank Holiday jolliness about it, and on Saturdays prefers not to go far, but today the air in her little room is fetid. The temperature has soared, young men in the street dressed in plimsolls and shorts, women in gay printed frocks with birch-brown legs and ankles. She had never seen so many ice-creams in so short a space of time. It was fresher in the park, the Saturday atmosphere quite unlike what she imagined it would be, and quite a different type of person to the few regulars she sees on her Tuesday visits, but of course they would be. On Tuesdays they are at work; on Saturdays they come to the park with their wives and children. The abundance of fellow creatures delights her for a while, but she soon tires of it, as if the consolations the park offers her on a Tuesday had been forever tarnished by the weekend uproar.

Mrs MacNiece must have been watching from the sitting-room window because no sooner has Dorothy opened the front door than the woman's there with a piece of paper in her hand.

'A telephone call,' says Mrs MacNiece accusingly. 'I was having my cheese on toast when the telephone rang. He was enquiring for Dolly. Of course, I told him no one of that name was at this address, but he insisted this was the number he had been given. He said the most extraordinary thing. He said, "I'm looking for the Doll with a Dimple."'

Chapter Seven

I

'If it had not been for the devoted attention of the son of the deceased, Mrs Makepeace's death would have been very different, and occurred many years earlier.'

Mervyn Brace, Deputy Coroner, leaned forward, as if whispering into the ears of those that sat, nonplussed by arcane procedure, across the courtroom.

'It would be remiss of me not to take this occasion to remark on the trauma that Heron Makepeace has suffered, and on the catalogue of near tragedies that has clouded his existence. In considering the circumstances of Mrs Belinda Makepeace's death, we must reflect on her history of attempted suicides, the details of which we have heard described by witnesses.

'We have learned how, when walking through a riverside park with her son, Mrs Makepeace was about to throw herself from a bridge into the water when her son alerted a passing stranger to help restrain her. We have heard from her next-door neighbour how, making an unscheduled call at the house, she was happily in time to rescue Mrs Makepeace from the kitchen, having discovered her already unconscious and with her head in the oven. Remarkably, it was the intervention of a quick-witted passenger on the London underground, restraining Mrs Makepeace as she flung herself from the platform at Tottenham Court Road into the path of an approaching train, that once again saved her from self-destruction.

'This was, alas, a path on which she was determined to continue. We have heard her sister tell the court that when Mrs Makepeace and her son spent a holiday with her in Shoreham last year, Mrs Makepeace expressed a wish to visit Beachy Head. The proposed excursion naturally set alarm bells ringing with Mrs Makepeace's son and sister, who were only too aware of her suicidal tendencies. In the event, they went instead on a railway journey, during which Mrs Makepeace, having excused herself from the carriage she shared with her son and sister, was found in the corridor with her head out of the window. Anxious as to why she had not returned to the carriage, Mr Makepeace searched the corridors for his mother. It was fortunate that another passenger, returning from the restaurant car, entered the corridor from the opposite direction. He and Mr Makepeace pulled her free of the window. A few moments later the train was due to enter a tunnel. Mrs Makepeace would undoubtedly have been decapitated.

'Having failed to take her own life with the co-operation of British Railways, it was but a few weeks later that Mrs Makepeace, driven out for the day by her son, was taken to Budderley Heights, a beauty spot known to walkers and climbers. Having parked the car safely at the peak of the hills, her son was laying the picnic he had prepared for them at the side of the car when he became aware that the vehicle was slowly moving downhill. Thankfully, another picnicker assisted him in bringing the vehicle to a halt, so that once again his mother was plucked from the mouth of catastrophe.

'We heard yesterday from the witness Mr Brenning that he was present at yet another of Mrs Makepeace's attempted suicides. A one-time member of the Cromer lifeboat crew, Mr Brenning happened to be in Cromer for a meeting that day. Mrs Makepeace and her son were holidaying in the town. Mr Brenning was passing along the sea front when he saw Mrs Makepeace apparently propelling herself into a storm-tossed sea.'

In fact, Mr Brenning had given the coroner quite a detailed account of the episode. When asked by Brace to describe what he had seen that day, Brenning glanced in Heron's direction to measure the degree of grief he was enduring, before pausing for thought and replying to the coroner.

'It all happened so quickly. So very quickly that I suppose I acted on instinct.'

'The instinct, presumably, of a lifeboatman?'

'Once you've been on the lifeboats, it's part of you.'

Like riding a bike, thought Heron, only wetter.

'Although, Mr Brenning, I believe you are now employed as a fireman in another county?'

'That is correct, yes.'

'From one admirable profession to another,' said Brace, almost bowing his head in reverence. 'And that life-saving instinct which is clearly an essential component of your character spurred you to help Mr Makepeace save his mother?'

'To save his mother?' Brenning's head was down, his eyes looking up at Heron. 'Well … naturally. Yes.'

'In your judgement, did you consider Mrs Makepeace to be attempting to take her own life?'

'Well …' Brenning mumbled.

'Could you speak up a little, Mr Brenning?'

'Like I said, it was all over in a flash. Soon as I came down towards the beach I saw the woman and the man were in danger. It was a pretty bad storm. The sea was broiling. I could see he was moving her wheelchair about …'

'To keep control of it, you mean?'

'I was still a little way off, and the rain was beating in my face.'

'I see.'

'What was clear was that she was in danger of being swallowed by the sea. It looked to me as if the man had hold of one of the wheelchair's handles. The visibility was bad. The weather was atrocious.'

'And it was this fact,' suggested the coroner, 'that perhaps suggested to Mrs Makepeace, intent as she apparently was (if we are to take into account the several other incidents we have learned of) on self-destruction, that this tempestuous weather might offer her an opportunity for self-annihilation?'

Brenning pushed his fingers against his beard at this moment, pushing his lips out as if thinking how to respond.

'Could be, yes. Perhaps a different person, someone a bit more with it, let's say, would have chosen a much simpler way of doing themselves in. I didn't think much of it at the time, but after it struck me you could find much easier ways of doing yourself in. She could have taken pills, or put too much water in the bath. I don't know. It just seemed a bit of a rigmarole to me, you know, the means not justifying the end, if you see what I mean.'

'I'm not altogether sure that I do, Mr Brenning.'

'Oh, and it was only after I'd called out to him as I came round the corner that I heard Mr Makepeace call for help.'

66

'That, I think, is understandable. After all, no matter how hard he may have called for assistance, the noise of the storm would have obliterated his voice.'

'Yes, that's what I thought,' said Brenning.

'Thank you. Your comments have been most helpful. I am sure the court and Mr Makepeace would like to express gratitude for the essential part you played in rescuing Mrs Makepeace from a watery grave. You are free to leave the court if you wish.'

Brenning almost slid out of the witness box, avoiding looking at the deceased's son as he made for the exit.

Mervyn Brace was thoroughly tired of the case. From the evidence, it seemed Mrs Makepeace was a miserable creature who had made almost a profession of wanting to end her life. At four o'clock, thinking of the whist party his wife had instructed him to be in good time for, he decided the court need hear no more.

'It must have come as a great relief to Mr Makepeace that, at the final counting, his mother died a natural death, passing at home in her sleep in her own bed in God's way. In recording the fact that she died from natural causes, we extend our deepest sympathy to Mr Makepeace.'

II

Heron could remember it still, word for word, almost, remembered the summery pepper in the air as he walked from the court into that springy morning, trees above him rustling at the coroner's words. It was just like people said, a weight lifted from your shoulders. He consigned it to the past with more ease than he'd imagined, as if all of it had happened to somebody else which, in a way, it had. Anyway, it was still what they called early days. Why did people put so much dependence on what other people said: 'it was just like they said', 'what they called early days', 'we extend our sympathy?'. Heron wanted to shuffle the words off, leave them behind in the courtroom, the meaningless kindness of neighbours, the obligatory sadness of relatives (not that there were any to come moping), the necessary words at his mother's graveside, the official condolences, the sympathy cards he'd torn up after a couple of days. It was a sort of gift from God, he thought, how he opened the front door when he got back from the court and the telephone was ringing. Pealing, he thought afterwards, announcing a new beginning, a salty renaissance by the sea. A decent boarding house, he was assured, and a professional return to the public gaze, and the management of Monty Desmond a feather in his cap.

He left Acton after listening to the eight o'clock news on the wireless, having booked for the ten o'clock coach at Victoria. Arriving half an hour early, he went into a chemist, remembering he had forgotten to pack shaving cream. As the assistant turned away to fetch the article from a shelf, Heron lifted a tin of fruit pastilles from the counter and slid them silently into his pocket. He dozed on the coach journey, intermittently sucking the pastilles and catching occasional blotches of landscape as he wavered between consciousness and oblivion. Setting down in Norwich, he waited another hour for a bus to Cromer. He felt the inside pocket of his tweed jacket, reassured that he hadn't forgotten his pension book.

'Mrs Freebody?' he said as she opened the door of Greenbanks.

He could see it was well maintained by the glisten of the privet. Apparently, he was the last to arrive. Mrs Freebody let out a gasp of relief. They had all been counted in, and all seemed respectable, none more than this man who looked as if he'd never said boo to a goose, and not a performing animal among them. His voice had the sound of a flute with a pea stuck in its insides. She would have been surprised to know he had been one of Ivor Novello's favourites, employing him over and over again for the male chorus of his musicals, just as he had Olive Gilbert. Olive, Ivor's very own Welsh Rarebit, had been Heron's best mate in those days. Mrs Freebody would find out more at breakfast, when the first hint of complaint usually surfaced, although those concerning pubic hair leftovers from previous visitors had never been aired when other guests were present.

Although he didn't know it, Heron's room was the tiniest of all, and the sun only popped in, when it was about, for a few minutes in the early morning. His hostess climbed the stairs with enough heaviness to suggest she wouldn't want to be going up and down them on his account ever again. She felt instinctively that she'd have no trouble with Mr Makepeace. It was an impression he easily gave, first impressions being so important and conveyed by his carefree pleasantness. For a moment, she heard him behind her softly whistling 'Roses Of Picardy'. It was a song his mother had always hated.

Chapter Eight

'**I** shall be in my room attending to my fan mail,' said Hattie. She hadn't received any in years, but you never gave up hoping, and it was the impression that counted. Lady Darting attempted to soften her crow-like features. The attempt was unsuccessful. Her first impression of her guest was unimpressive, and she had landed herself with the woman for three weeks. It was like being the commander of a requisitioned depot.

'Not to worry,' said Hattie, lifting her head and tossing it as she did when making a point. 'I won't be in your way. The lightest of breakfasts, and for the next three days I'll be at the theatre all day.'

Lady Darting had looked forward to giving the woman a conducted tour of the Hall, and the retelling of Uncle Remus' expedition through the Greater Algerian Pass was always well received. As it was, Hattie had merely glanced to where her hostess's long-dead uncle stood, canvas-fixed, beside an alarmingly short native. Usually, sight of the portrait sparked a fascinating discussion about the history of the pygmy race, but Lady Darting had overlooked the fact that Hattie Prince had never conspicuously showed the slightest interest in other people. Hattie's conversational skills depended on her bringing round any other subject under discussion back to herself. Once launched, the list of her seemingly endless achievements and triumphs was rolled out and relished.

Even now, with the crow-like face still talking, Hattie floated away from the woman's voice. She wasn't convinced the woman knew anything about her, hadn't a clue who she was, or what she had been. It was a state of affairs that could not be allowed to continue. Although it seemed to her hostess that Hattie was oblivious to the surroundings she found herself in, she was not. She was acutely conscious of where she had come from, and the never-ending necessity for pride.

If asked for details of her past she gave them, to the reporters, the fans who seldom wrote letters, anyone who would listen. Her beginning hadn't involved marble halls. The two-up two-down terraced family home was only four dead cows' length from the slaughterhouse where the baying of the doomed beasts interrupted the cries of children playing in the street, muddling up the sounds until you thought the children were mooing and the cows at hopscotch. Her father was a black-face comic, a never-ending laundry problem for his wife, always at the scrub-brush, berating the day he'd seen a minstrel troupe and thought he could do as much. Hattie and Enid were born two years apart, Hattie first, in the upstairs bedroom among the bugs. 'More hot water!' the doctor kept screaming. He'd be lucky. It was hard enough to fetch the cold carried up from the yard, let alone hot. All those years ago. Hattie worked it out on her fingers. She was 86 now, standing where her mum and dad would never have believed, the guest of aristocracy.

They didn't need to know everything about her dad. Hattie overlooked, painted the genteelest of pictures, how he'd put her on his knee and taught her songs, piccaninny songs, odd when she came to think of it because 'Piccadilly Lily' was in the same vein, and had been her bread-and-butter number for all these years, the one people demanded of her, picking up the chorus.

'One Step Forward, Two Steps Back', that was one of the first she'd sung, not too bad when you needed a decent booking before a competent songwriter would agree to write a number for you. 'Oh, let me do it, daddy' she'd cry, doing the steps he'd shown her, altering them here and there, adding her particular dash of charm. The way she told it, it had been a childish delight, no mention of the woman that dad had got in charge of her, a stick and a back hand if she put a foot or hand wrong on stage, and she was on it by the age of six, 'Little Moira', dubiously treated by the woman her father had put his trust in. Marie Lloyd had stepped in, one night when Little Moira had got something close to the bird at the Oxford, to protect her. In her long career, it was one of the very few acts of kindness Hattie could recall.

It was strange when you thought of it, her golden hair streaming down her back, just as it streamed still. People wondered that she didn't have an Eton crop, after all she was always complaining it took her hours to pin up, but Hattie clung to her femininity. The contradiction did not occur to her. She was still a young woman, in her late teens, when she ordered the little naval suit and shirts and collars and cuff-links and studs and a watch-chain and monocle and waistcoats and trousers and spats and jackets and bowlers and opera capes and opera hats and patent leather shoes and all sorts of men's titfers and white gloves and silk scarves and a regular carnation for the buttonhole and cigars and cigarettes and pipes and Bryant and May matches and sticks. She put away the childish things, the pretty dresses and frills. Now, the make-up no longer enhanced, but transformed, her. These trappings would be the paraphernalia to see her through life, indeed they became it. Just as the memory of Little Moira had long faded from the minds of her audiences, it faded from her own, and Hattie Prince took her place.

Of course, Lady Darting must be made aware of Hattie's past, her successes in the States, her name as high as however tall skyscrapers were being built in 1905, and in Australia, where she'd been feted by society's elite and uncouth gold prospectors alike, endlessly photographed and filmed standing jolly and matey among working people, in all but truth one of them, slapping her fellow-men on the back, sharing racy nudges.

Returning to London, she'd recruited boys for the Great War, few able to resist her rendition of 'Don't Cry, Just Wave Goodbye', one of those songs that, as in legend, really had been whistled by errand-boys and even, most probably, in the trenches listening out for a whizz-bang. She'd sung it from the deck of a ship bearing the boys away to France, them joining in the chorus, dead fags at the corner of their young mouths, leaving England for the first and last time. A doctor had made her stop signing her photographs, fearing for her wrist, and she'd been copied, her signature printed into the picture. The boys went on believing she'd signed it just for them.

She does not speak of the men she knew best. Husbands, three of them: Henry Baldock, illusionist and supposed hypnotist, whom she had divorced in 1928, The Honourable Clarence Thorogood who had behaved as every high-born Stage Door Johnny of the period behaved, ultimately leaving her for a blowsy showgirl, and third time unlucky Roland Carwithick who switched his attention to a male dancer at Sadler's Wells. At some time in each of their post-Hattie lives all three husbands used the words 'lucky escape'.

One of her rare off-stage talents – for she was a shocking housekeeper, and seldom allowed anyone other than Enid into her Covent Garden baggage-room of a flat – was to put the past where it belonged, behind her. Unlike others, and of course she was quite unlike them, she had somehow always belonged to the times, going on as others fell away. Poor Lottie Collins had died when only forty-four, in 1910 (and there was a year she'd never forget), probably exhausted by her 'Ta-ra-ra-boom-de-ay'. When Lottie first sang it she'd fainted twice from fatigue. Ida Barr, quite a different class of artist to Hattie, had been big in every sense in 1910, but couldn't ride out the ragtime phase. She'd seen Ida at a charity do a few months ago, vulgar as ever, reminding the house what audiences used to say of her, 'Ida Barr? She could hide a bleedin' pub', and then going into 'Oh, You Beautiful Doll'.

Lord Darting, thrilled at the prospect of welcoming a male impersonator to the Hall, had withdrawn to his room after his wife had introduced him to Hattie. He reappeared at tea-time, his entrance stage-managed by Lady Darting. As he wafted into the cavernous drawing-room in a haze of chiffon, the highest of heels at his lowest point and a magnificent blonde bouffant at his highest, his bony frame supported on silk-stockinged legs, Lady Darting turned with a flourish to where her husband stood.

'And this, Miss Prince, is Lady Cynthia.'

Hattie stared, her eyes widening.

'I regret to inform you,' she said, 'that I do not approve of transvestites.'

CHAPTER NINE

I

'I do wish you'd settle.'

In Cromer, Elsie was dizzy from the way Perry was moving around Mrs Freebody's premises, standing up, looking from the window, sitting down, opening the door to the hall, peering around the corner, up and down.

'It proves the point,' she said. 'We were stuck in a groove. We'd left the past behind. Perry! You're not listening to me.'

There was no doubt of it, so there was no need for him to agree. Anyway, that was what you did with the past, let it be. He'd never wanted to come to Cromer. The groove suited him. The new worries, that he wouldn't be able to wheel her into the town, up and down the bloody pier, that she'd have a turn and the doctor wouldn't be the one who knew how up and down her health was, and how she manipulated those around her, how he'd manage to shift her bulky, unmoving body around the stage, and what Mrs Freebody's food was like. Something about Mrs Freebody, wide smiles as she'd welcomed them and waved at various highlights of the house, suggested it wouldn't be cordon bleu. Catering to Elsie's culinary demands had taken him years to master. Being a seaside town, he thought they might be offered shellfish, lobsters and parts of an octopus, and whelks and winkles as part of a high tea, none of which would be suitable for Elsie, although a nice piece of plaice would have been acceptable if carefully poached. He was sure this wasn't the sort of establishment that dished up cod, though the corridors smelled of its relatives. When he opened the door to the hall, leftovers of forgotten meals wafted in, soggy and salty and disagreeable, coming vaguely from where he imagined Mrs Freebody's kitchen was situated, behind a sign that said 'Private', but it was other worries that predominated.

The thing was, he said to Elsie as he at last made the effort to calm himself, they hadn't been told who else was in the show. He'd seen posters as they arrived in Cromer, but the taxi was travelling too fast for him to read them. They had some idea. Cavan O'Connor had been mentioned as the top-liner, and Elsie had pulled a face, having worked with him once on Bournemouth Pier. She was then mobile, able to nip out of the way easily, just as well in the circumstances. Please God it wouldn't be him.

When he'd first rung them, Monty had spoken of Dorothy Driscoll in glowing terms, asking if Elsie or Perry knew of her whereabouts. Elsie put on her unenthusiastic voice.

'I thought she was dead,' she'd told him.

'I saw her once,' Monty had said, a faraway look in his voice, and it almost choked, 'in a tour of *Rose Marie*. Magic, she was. Sheer magic.'

Elsie tilted her head sympathetically. She kept it secret that no one had ever, to her knowledge, said as much of her. It niggled her again, sitting in a corner of this boarding house in Cromer into which Perry had with difficulty tucked her. Mrs Freebody had overseen their progress from garden path to room, noting that the wheelchair almost scraped the paintwork. The shape of their room made it necessary for Elsie's vehicle to be wedged into an oblong recess, well away from the window. Perry made up for this by leaning forward to get a better view of what was happening in the street, and of who might ring the doorbell.

'An old man,' he said, pinning himself at the edge of a wall, 'by the look of him, a very old man, and a younger one. They drew up in a van.'

Another time, he pulled the door open to catch an exchange between Mrs Freebody and another elderly man, stouter, in a trilby and wool coat. Although he heard few words, he was conscious of the man's ill-fitting teeth and a hissing sound as if someone had left a hosepipe on the go. Mrs Freebody addressed him as Mr Makepeace. By the end of the day Perry thought he'd counted in most of the arrivals, and hadn't recognised any.

Their afternoon lapsed into anxiety. Grenville and Elsie hadn't had to worry about the professional competition since they had retired in 1945. Now, Elsie needed to rest if they were to attend the welcoming sherry party Mrs Freebody was giving that evening in her drawing room, usually out of bounds to guests. Dinner would have been more welcome, Perry thought but didn't say, but bed and breakfast had been what they'd expected. All day, the house had squeaked and bumped through the hours, the doorbell going, wardrobes banging, opening and closing, drawers pulled and pushed, hangers clanging softly in the plywood semi-dark, switches pressed on and (more welcome to Mrs Freebody) off. It was a place suddenly restless, a virus of apprehension spreading through it, nervous of what tomorrow would bring and how jolly the sherry party might be. Experience, a dull deep feeling within them, had turned Grenville and Elsie into glum, elderly gladiators unsure of which of them would win the day, a sense of old wounds threatening to gape, a reawakening of dozing suspicions. Oh, fill 'em up, fill 'em up, fill 'em up, it is my birthday! Let us all remain, there's plenty of old champagne, fill 'em up and put 'em down and fill 'em up again. Don't stop! Don't stop! I love to hear the corks go pop, pop, pop, the sound that makes us all feel gay. One never knows, does one, what may happen to a mother's son before his next birthday?

In fact, the sherry party went off better than any of the guests expected, except for Mrs Freebody who knew the way of these occasions: when the bottle of sherry was empty, it was over. She had poured timid amounts of the liquid into large tumblers, aware of the age of her guests and the possibilities of tremor and spillage. They'd hardly got into the room and were clutching their drinks when Perry and Elsie (parked behind an aspidistra) discovered the identity of the star turn. Hattie Prince! A ripple of nervous laughter, a spluttering of sherry, a 'Well, I never'.

'We were told Cavan O'Connor,' said Elsie, hoping to get her account of her Bournemouth experience into the conversation. It would at least have alerted those present to the inadvisability of ever being with a man in a closed space.

The old man staying with the younger man didn't come down. The journey had taken the stuffing out of him, Henry had told Mrs Freebody, better for him to rest. At this news, the image of the younger man sitting by the old man's bed above them somehow fixed in their minds. Dorothy Driscoll refused the sherry, so Mrs Freebody had to go through the door marked 'Private' to fetch a glass of squash that tasted mostly of water. Elsie's realisation that Dorothy was not dead was not received with the wonder she had anticipated. Parliamentary

Pete settled in a corner, having announced that it was his right leg they had to watch out for, although none could make out if this was his real one or the false one donated by the National Health Service. At least, one leg stuck out at an angle from where he sat taking sudden nips of the sherry.

Heron Makepeace didn't say much, stood about in the way of a cupboard from which Mrs Freebody had to ask him to move because she wanted a timetable (Dolly meant to use her bus pass while she was in the area), and then had to get up from a chair because a photograph of Mr Freebody was on a shelf above him and she couldn't reach. Passed from hand to hand in a silver frame, Mr Freebody smiled up at them as if this was the expression he would have worn had he been there in the flesh, which in the circumstances was not possible, and which if it had been possible he would have avoided. Heron, who had never liked moustaches, didn't like the look of him. Any social do alarmed Heron, prone as he was to over-excitement, and then his voice went into a falsetto that turned heads. He didn't take to the man with the odd leg, either, preferring that the medical upset had not been mentioned, and the leg in question (whichever one it was) aligned with the other, not protruding into the room. The woman in the wheelchair, introduced to him as Miss Balls, had almost jumped up when Heron's voice, as it unexpectedly did, changed gear. He wondered at the days ahead, how he would put up with these dreadful people.

He didn't let on that he knew Cromer. Mother and he had holidayed here often, staying in the upper reaches of the little town at the Cliftonville, to which they had returned twice a year, once in early spring and once in autumn when the gardens along the cliff top were at their quietest, the petunias going off. It would seem odd, being here without her. Even when infirm, she had loved it, the stiff breeze blowing in from the North Sea, morning coffee at the Tudor Tea Rooms, dinner at the hotel for which she insisted on dressing, her black lace and rope of pearls maintaining a standard that other diners marvelled at, even when she, like Elsie Balls, was stuck in a wheelchair and the cutlery always needed a once-over with a napkin.

The last time they stayed in Cromer, their final holiday, she hadn't let the immobility affect her, her spirit undimmed, her sense of adventure unaltered. She'd always been fascinated by the lifeboats, always spoken of at Cromer. It wouldn't have surprised him if she'd wished for a tragedy at sea, just so she could have seen the men in their sou'westers, the rain lashing weather-beaten faces as they carved through the waves to her rescue. There was a gale blowing the day she insisted on going to where the lifeboats were. Mother and son, pushing their way against the biting wind and spume towards where the lifeboats lived. It was her idea to get close up, although he could never quite explain how it was she had got onto the slipway, en route to the sea. His protestations that it wasn't safe couldn't be heard above the crashing magnificence of the storm. Perhaps the wheels of her chair skidded on the slippery slope, his hand missed the handle, she leaned too far as if to reach into the depths of the water, but the chair had begun to move, gathering speed with frightening force.

They took him into the lifeboat men's quarters after, brandy for him and mum because of the shock, and the next day it got into the papers. Heron wasn't surprised. It wasn't often that lifeboat men were responsible for saving a life on dry land. A moment later and Mrs Makepeace would probably have been lost in, if not at, sea, if it hadn't been for the lifeboatman who happened to be passing. The storm had come on so quickly.

The son, battered and blinded by the raging tempest, had simply lost control of his mother's wheelchair. The newspaper recognised that the speed of the passing lifeboatman's actions and the woman's son had saved the day. They asked Heron for a photograph to go on the front page, but he declined, putting on the face of a bashful hero.

II

Every morning on waking at Cromer Glynis thought of Sister Agathe. Once it had always been in colour, with the sound of her voice attached, now it was the shade and texture of an old print, and silent. It was Sister Agathe to whom Glynis was responsible in the convent, the elder woman having oversight of the vegetables that provided so vital a component of the nun's diet. If you asked her, Agathe would tell you her history, which was not always the case with nuns, so often keeping their past locked away, and she was not the most popular among the other nuns, perhaps because of this. She wasn't Irish, either, which didn't help, and never shy of explaining she was an outsider who might have become a bus conductress, a teacher of young children or a campaigner of some sort. The other nuns didn't understand why with such a choice of careers Agathe had turned her face from the world and entered St Gertrude's, and were unsure of her commitment to a common cause. Her friendship with Glynis aligned her more with the outside world than the one made up within the walls of St Gertrude's, and the suspicion that she belonged in two worlds rather than one distanced Sister Agathe from her fellows. In time she was thought of as a woman who could not make up her mind, and whose stay in the convent might be temporary.

Glynis had come there one day in a long-ago February, a bad weather winter when the snow persisted week on week, her mother concerned that the women on the hill might be in difficulty. The convent was known to be Spartan, no heating but the one great fire in the communal dining room that depended on logs, and so far as they knew no vehicle had got through the choked roads. Her father couldn't see that it mattered. This was the life the women had chosen, this was the place they had decided to live it in, it was they who had cut themselves off, with no consideration for anyone who lived outside, shutting themselves away in the belief that God would provide. Now was His chance to prove them right, but Glynis had the boots and wanted to climb the hill. They were a Christian family, after all, her mother argued, and no harm would be done. She and Glynis packed a basket with bread fresh from the oven, cheese and milk, because Gideon Murphy was still managing to deliver from the grocer in the village. Her mother was for including a copy of the local newspaper so the nuns would know what was going on. Let them know about the wider world, she said, but they decided against it. After all, as Glynis' father pointed out, the women had no telephone, so they must assume they wouldn't be interested in current affairs.

There was a room where, as it were, the outside world and the enclosed one the nuns inhabited, met, a small oblong of space, with a slot of a high window from which light bent itself in as if from heaven, its colour shifting through cloud and sunlight. Glynis waited at the door, too long for any eventual response to be encouraging, but it opened at last and there was Sister Agathe, her hands floury, a dab of the stuff at her cheek. It was always Sister Agathe who opened the door on every subsequent visit Glynis made. That first time, she told

Glynis how pleased the Mother Superior would be to have this show of kindness, and she was to return home with the news that everything was well at the convent, that they had food and light and warmth, there being no cause for concern. God was not mentioned specifically, but hung, unspoken, around them. Had Glynis been more inquisitive, she might have been disappointed not to be allowed into the convent itself, but only into the little room with the high window, whose glass was golden, so disappointed that she wouldn't bother to return. But from that first moment, when Sister Agathe indicated the girl might sit opposite her in the room, across the square brown table with a crucifix at its centre, Glynis was content, felt herself in some way bettered. Information was relayed from the Mother Superior that she was deeply grateful for the kind thoughts the girl had brought to the place. Encouraged by this, Sister Agathe said she hoped that Glynis would call again, call again when the snow had melted, when the journey from the village was less arduous.

It was odd how it happened, but the next day the snow had gone by late morning, the sun burning it away from the paths and hills, and out of the fields where Glynis had to pass Mrs Riley's farm where the deformed pig with wonky ankles always turned to stare at her as she went by, its squinting eye weeping. Glynis' mother watched her too, her daughter starting up the hill to the convent. It was then, her second visit to the little room, that Glynis noticed its whiteness, virginal and intense.

Chapter Ten

I

'Oh, I do like to be beside the seaside!'
    'Beside the seaside?'
'Beside the sea. When you're strolling by the ocean.'
'The ocean? What a commotion!'
'All the girls are lovely by the seaside. All the girls are lovely by the sea. All their frills and bits of finery!'
'I do love to stroll along the prom, prom, prom.'
'Where the brass bands play? Tiddley om pom pom!'
'Sweet Saturday night, when your week's work is over, that's the evening you make a throng, take your dear little girls along.'
'Sweet Saturday night! But this hour is Monday morning. To work you must go, though longing, I know, for sweet Saturday night.'
'Last summertime,' a man in a striped swimming suit is telling them, 'I went away to Hemsby by the sea, and thought I'd like to bring a piece of seaweed home with me.'
They're not all of them listening, some leaning over and pointing at the waves, counting how fast they tumble on the shore, some holding hands, promises whispered, some

treasured, few kept. In the twilight, in the twi twilight, in the twi twi twilight, out in the beautiful twilight, they all go out for a walk, walk, walk, a quiet old spoon and a talk, talk, talk, and some (one too many) go home doing the wibbley wobbley walk. That's the time they long for, just before the night, and many a grand little wedding is planned in the twilight, the twi twilight, in the twi twi twilight of Cromer Pier, which after all is a structure and has no sense of its past, and the songs that lay about it still, the poems of pierrots, the nonsenses of red-nose comics, the thighs of old dancing girls, once young in net and tulle. The ones who don't listen watch and listen elsewhere, thinking of ships, dots on the water's horizon.

'She has a sailor for a lover,' whispers one of them, his summery eyes turning to where a girl stands at the sea-end of the pier, a figurehead leaning to the wind and oceans beyond.

'It tells you if it's going to rain,' says the man with the seaweed.

'Or if it's going to snow?'

'All the girls are lovely by the seaside. All the girls are lovely by the sea. All the nice girls love a sailor. Oh, all the nice girls love a tar.'

'There's something about a sailor. You know what sailors are!'

'Bright and breezy?'

'Free and easy. They're the ladies' pride and joy. Fall in love with Kate and Jane, and it's off to sea again, ship ahoy! ship ahoy!'

'Oh, just let me be beside the seaside, I'd be beside myself with glee. There's lots of girls beside I should like to be beside, beside the seaside, beside the sea.'

There's a little crowd now, wanting to hear more about the man who took the seaside home with him, like the seaside posters round the home.

'With my seaweed in my hand, I hopped into the train. All the pubs were closed when I got out again. I couldn't get a drink, with thirst I thought I'd die, and as soon as I touched my seaweed, I knew it was going to be dry!'

Some dream of home, still, or the night their love burst free, leaning over the ironwork, the sound of the sea assuring them that this was how it started, and why it goes on still, wave after wave. A young man, his natty get-up dampening in the salt breeze, remembering, asking, hoping his girl hadn't yet forgotten that night in May, down at the Welsh Harp which is Hendon way. She'd whispered 'Winkles, and a pot of tea', but 'Four 'alves' he'd murmured, 'good enough for me'. Oh, he'd cried, 'Give me a word of hope that I may win.' She prods him gently with her winkle-pin. Oh, they were so happy that day, down at the Welsh Harp which is Hendon way. The young Hendon lad, even damper after getting through the chorus, breathes deep, enriched, exhilarated by the mere act of being on the pier, for one week only a lion comique, he might be the George Leybourne of Cromer and sing out George's commands 'Night Is The Time To Have A Spree, My Boys', and prove that all the girls don't necessarily love a sailor, if he can wait till the twi twi twilight, and quite a few of the boys wouldn't object to it either. And oh, oh, oh the choice!

Those girls, those girls, those lovely seaside girls, with sticks they steer and promenade the pier to give the boys a treat, in pique silks and lace they tip you quite a playful wink.

'Wink the other eye!'

'Those girls, those girls, those lovely seaside girls, all dimples, smiles and curls, your head it simply whirls! They look all right, complexions pink and white, they've diamond rings and dainty feet, golden hair from Regent Street, lace and grace and lots of face, those pretty little seaside girls!'

The man with the story to tell plods on. 'It tells you if it's going to rain or if it's going to snow, and with it anyone can tell just what he wants to know.'

'Oh?'

'With my seaweed in my hand, like I said, all the pubs were closed when I got out again. I couldn't get a drink, with thirst I thought I'd die, and as soon as I touched my seaweed I knew it was going to be dry.'

The weather's changeable, of course, even by the sea. 'He kissed her ruby lips,' he's telling them, 'and looked at her with pride. He said, I shall be glad when, darling, you're my bride. Tomorrow we'll be wed,' he says, 'and then you will be mine', and as soon as he touched his seaweed he knew it was going to be fine.'

There's those who don't bother, of course, stayaways, keep-at-homes who can't be doing with the brine and the ice-creams and knick-knackery and the paper hats and smutty postcards, making do with seaside posters round the home. They're the type that never want to journey by the foam! There's Brighton in the bathroom and papa feels quite a swell because he cuts his corns outside the Metropole Hotel. They have Plymouth in the pantry and there's Yarmouth in the yard and Bournemouth they keep somewhere in the back, and in the little parlour where the ladies sit and chat they've got Clacton with the accent on the clac!

II

It's a grand little procession, this sunny September morning, its components just about moving as one, conscious that lookers-on will know they have a purpose, the purpose being to reach the end of the pier and the stage door without incident or need of oxygen tent. One wheelchair and various problematic limbs (one leg known to be missing) are involved. The Revd Challis, Cromer's theatrical chaplain, leads them on, prayer book in hand, the sense of occasion paramount on this God-given morning, the geriatric column having been transported en masse from Mrs Freebody's. The Revd Challis is profoundly moved today as he is on all occasions involving the elderly out and about, and these, after all, are remarkable specimens, well past the excitement of first receiving their pension books. Even as they dismounted the bus (really a miniature coach, as if the passengers had been collected from Toytown, with massive chromium bumpers that gleamed in the autumn light), a small crowd formed at the forefront of the pier. Something unmistakably theatrical was afoot, and the Revd Challis, his face recognised from his role in the Branlingham Parsnip Scandal, like them played the innocent bystander. As if in acknowledgement of the riotous spirit of the disreputable old music-halls, shameless middle-aged women revealing several inches of intimate hosiery had obligingly placed themselves on the public seating lining the edges of the pier. The danger of their breaking into song was apparent to all, so infectious the occasion, so reckless the effect of the stabbing heat of intermittent sunshine.

The potential vulgarity appalled Heron Makepeace. At this moment his life's ambition was to reach the end of the pier, slip into the stage door and become what he had once been, an echo of the lost world of Ivor Novello, but this being Cromer the fear was that he might run into a lifeboatman, a member of the crew, indeed the very descendent of Henry Blogg that had rescued – or, more accurately, helped him to rescue – his mother from the foaming brine. Should he bump into him, although it was more likely the man would be out shrimping or sitting at the edge of the shingle, his wide eyes scanning the horizon for another disaster, he would apologise for the bother his mother had caused. As Heron had told the coroner, she had mounted to little more than a continuous nuisance to the authorities with her repeated attempts at suicide, suggesting that it would have been preferable had she long ago, for her own safety, been committed to an institution for the criminally insane. The fat ladies revealing too much underwear on either side of the pier gaze at Heron, tubby and ridiculously dapper in his tight blue blazer – the brass buttons straining to get away – white slacks and tennis shoes, the striped tie the remnant of a cricket club do. Mother liked him neatly turned out.

Peregrine Grenville pushed Elsie Balls to the head of the queue. She had taken particular trouble with her hair, the grey slightly blue, an impression of light froth about her head. Her wheelchair grated across the wooden struts of the pier, making it seem that its occupant was having a bad fit of hiccups, but Elsie gloried in it. No wheelchair but a chariot, bearing her on to a revival of the life she had known in the spotlight. Perry had already grazed his knee against the steel wheels, and went into a hobble. Tits and teeth, he thought, essential now, just as his leg buckled. Oh, song was in the air, airs in the air rising from nowhere, the fat ladies and their worryingly thin friends, the bean-pole grow-your-own-sweet-peas-up-them, joining in, elbowing their neighbours into another chorus. Oh, give us another song, George, and if you're Irish come into the parlour and we'll sing of the green, or at the old Bull and Bush, come, come, come and make eyes at me at the old Bull and Bush. Half-remembered, misremembered, best forgotten, fugues of old melodies come and go as the parade passes by.

Dorothy Driscoll follows up, strangely apart. The end of the pier, the stage door, might as well be an execution shed, just when her life was settling, dad in the home, digs sorted. This wasn't what old age was meant to be, being shown off like a chimpanzee at the circus, and since Harry had gone, taking the money (not that there had been much of that) with him, what was left to her? It wasn't his fault. Nothing had ever been Harry's fault, not even her being reduced to two weeks on a pier at the arse's end of a summer season.

Oh God, she thought, if I turn this or that way they'll see the crack in the cheek, those watching faces of what they laughingly called the General Public – and she tries to block the faces oh those ugly faces out as she strides on, her shoes biting into her heels, the bald patch in the hair, the frayed hem, the discoloured petticoat, the arthritic finger, the lapsed bosom. Oh, with Harry at her side, she'd have had his hand in hers, and him saying 'You're fine, old girl. Bloody fine. We'll have one soon as we get there.'

And then, the miracle, a minor one, but a miracle of sorts.

'Excuse me, love,' calls a woman, 'aren't you Dorothy Driscoll?'

Well, it's only polite that Dorothy should stop in her tracks, one eye out for an autograph book. It's like she'd always believed, your performance starts as soon as you step into the street. They're there, unknown to you, the fans, the admirers from afar, the people who wonder all sorts of things about you, do things every day because of you, measure the other people in their lives (more fool them) against their image of you. This woman takes her hand, speaks of Skegness, and the Pleasure Gardens at Vauxhall where she'd seen Dorothy sing before the war. 'Oh, before the bombs! I'm talking well before the blitz' the woman cries, believing that a national tragedy shared is a national tragedy halved. She mentions doodlebugs, goes on about it.

'I remember what you sang,' the woman cries, mixing this up with a description of Hitler's menace, and on cue Dorothy twists slightly away, give me space, let my hands express what should be around me, let me make my own magic with no impediment of scenery or lights or props, and the woman, now slightly embarrassed to have taken things so far, sinks back to watch Dorothy go into her song, thinking of Mr Churchill and trying to imagine him without a cigar.

'Oh, it's all right in the summertime,' Dorothy sings, as those ahead of her in the procession get a little more ahead and look back to see what the commotion she is causing is all about, and now Dorothy is swinging an arm, simpering, perching beside the woman on the ironwork seat, crossing a leg across her knee, her finger under her chin – after all, she's the doll with the dimple.

'In the summertime, it's lovely,' croons Dorothy. 'My old man is painting hard, while I'm posing in the old back yard. But oh, oh, in the wintertime, it's another thing you know! With a little pink nose and very little clothes, and the wintry winds do blow!'

There's more than a spattering of applause at Dorothy's impromptu command performance, at the command of the Great British Public or its representatives on the pier. Oh,

Harry, perhaps Cromer wasn't such a bad idea after all, perhaps it's happiness. It would be Harry, oh how good it would be, you here with me. That would have been my happiness.

Dorothy's moment stops the procession's traffic, holding up Henry who's in Eastern garb, Turkish slippers and a turban, not everyday Cromer wear as some of the more observant onlookers comment. There's no denying Henry, despite his advanced years, has what used to be known as bearing, a back ramrod straight, an overall sense of control and no-nonsense about him. Trailing at his side, Len looks more ridiculous, but he's still young, and that's enough for some of the old ladies looking on from amongst their glimpses of undergarments and several of the younger ladies too, and he's wearing a sort of Egyptian blouse, see-through, pantaloons that come to just below his knees and what's left is enough to send some of the old dears back to their night's lodgings with fantasies raging, and his turban is crooked on top of his head and his shirt exposing too much of his chest and nipples as if he hasn't had time to readjust it after an amorous encounter in a harem. That night, in the privacy of their Cromer rooms his onlookers remember Len, and wonder what lies beneath.

'Oh God,' prays the Revd Challis, his little party having bowed their heads or looked through squinting eyes at the blinding sun, 'thank you for this day. We pray for the company of performers gathered before you, and that their time in Cromer will be one of harmony. We pray that those whom time has not wearied will bring joy and content to the holidaymakers. We know, God, that you as much as anyone appreciate the innocence of such delight.'

Oh yes, thinks Heron, there's nothing God enjoys more than a bit of a knees up.

'We thank you, God, that our performers have been blessed to live another day. As they enter this sea-girt Temple of Thespis let merriment and joy be conjured up at their behest. We ask for your blessing on this enterprise, confident that you will look sympathetically on *Forget-Me-Not*, ask your blessing on the cast, on the staff of Cromer Pier, on the cleaners and stewards, on the healing hands of the St John Ambulance Brigade who, due to the very considerable ages of those involved, will need to be at maximum alertness. How very true that they will be waiting in the wings! And so, as we stand here before you, about to harmonise with one another to bring music and laughter to the people of Cromer and its holidaymakers, we feel the sun's radiant ray shining down on us, a sign that all will be well.'

It was then the heavens opened. The carefree summeryness of the early autumn afternoon was wiped out as a gale careered along the length of the pier, the battering rain sending the reverend's little procession scurrying each and any direction in search of shelter. Slithering and slipshodding, the old caught their breath, fighting against the wind and hail, snapping on pacamacs, battling umbrellas already inside out, open-toed sandals at flood level, pixie-hoods unleashed from their tether, spectacles misted until they didn't know who was who or where the missus had gone, sandwiches dampened, squelching ice cream cones pulped. Seeking refuge in the Temple of Thespis, the Revd Challis shouted above the King-Learing storm, though the din was so intense that none heard.

He might as well have called 'Sanctuary!' as he beat on the stage door, but there was no response, the rain beating at the door as hard as the Revd Challis. The storm had driven everyone from its centre, as if a Red Sea had divided, leaving a wide avenue through the length of the pier. The star of the occasion could not have picked a better moment to appear, as she now did at the pier's entrance. The sky poured from where heaven was meant to be, the rain in every nook, the wind in any available cranny. There were few that day on Cromer Pier that forgot it, for there, soaked to the skin, stood Hattie Prince. Impeccably dressed as always, she tipped her top hat to the side of her head, lit a cigarette with infinite graciousness and, acknowledging the stares of the crowd with imperious confidence, walked on through them all. At that moment, the sun blazed across town and sea, more splendid than any could have imagined, as Hattie burst into a chorus of 'Piccadilly Lily'.

She had weathered every storm ever tossed at her, and would weather this one. When she reached the stage door it opened, as if by magic.

CHAPTER ELEVEN

I

The next day, Hattie was strolling past the Honey Pot Tea Room adjacent to the Hotel de Paris when the stranger approached her. She had glimpsed him sitting in the window of the little café, turning the pages of a magazine, but she almost started as he rose quickly from his chair, as if he had not been passing the time but waiting for her to appear, and rushed up to her in the street.

'Miss Prince?'

He must have been in his sixties, a little shabbily dressed, the bristles on his chin yesterdays, and Hattie always looked at the shoes.

'Yes?' she said, half acknowledging, half questioning, but always delighted to be recognised, and in public too, with others around to witness it.

'You won't know me. No reason why you should. I was on the pier when you arrived,' he said, 'but you had such a press of admirers around you, I wouldn't have dreamed of interrupting. What an occasion it was.'

'They gave us a very nice welcome,' said Hattie, generously recognising that there had been others beside herself receiving the municipal welcome, nodding her head in that vaguely charming but authoritative manner she had.

'I hope you'll come and see the show,' she said. In a moment he'd get out an autograph book and then, with a flourish, she'd be off, the richer by knowing the public loved her still. She'd learned years ago not to linger too long with fans.

'Would you care to join me for coffee?'

She'd been caught that way before, ended up paying for it too, and once a three-course lunch.

'That's kind of you, but I'm on my way to the theatre.'

'At this time of day?'

It was ten o'clock in the morning, after all.

'Then I won't delay you. Funnily enough, I was talking about you to some of the others congregated on the pier and they simply wouldn't credit it.'

'I'm sorry?'

'That you've been on the stage since you were six.'

Well, there was no denying it, though she was surprised that anyone knew such a fact. The surprise deepened as the man began reeling off more of them, the first time she'd sung 'I'm a Tiddly Wink Girl' and the theatre she'd sung it in, and who else was on the bill that week, and which theatre she'd gone to the week after, and how her father had worked black face.

'It must have been marvellous to play alongside Albert Chevalier at the Tivoli in 1914,' he said, getting into his stride, 'March I think it was – you'd just done a week in Barnstable – when he was doing his 'Alice, an East End Ecstasy' and you were singing 'Tell Me The Teeniest Thing'. What a number that was. You haven't sung it for years, have you? Of course, it was before you turned to the male impersonation. It was by W. P. Mosgrove and Percy Birstow if memory serves me. They wrote numbers for Ada Reeve, too, I think, but her stuff hasn't lasted like yours. Nothing like as sturdy.'

Well, Hattie couldn't swear to any of it but it sounded about right. Good God, the man knew more about her career than she did!

'Just imagine! In 1909 when you were singing 'Going My Way, Old Chum?' at the Bedford Music-Hall, Walter Sickert was painting Little Dot Hetherington, and a year later everyone was singing 'Let's All Go Down The Strand' although there didn't seem much point going down it because Gatti's was turned into a cinema in 1910 ...'

'Ah. The cinema! Not to mention the television!' said Hattie, hinting that this had represented an unconquerable blow to the art to which she had given her life.

'I was telling the others last night how your anniversary is coming up, too.'

'What anniversary?'

'"Piccadilly Lily". You first sang it at the Chepstow Grand in September 1907. Exactly fifty years ago! They don't write songs like that any more.'

'No, I don't believe they do.'

'What stories you could tell! It's a wonder you haven't written a book.'

Hattie put her head to one side as if this had of course been considered, as if publishers were constantly pestering her, and would prove of great interest to the public; it was just that she hadn't got around to writing it yet.

'You must be one of the very last of the great music-hall stars,' he said.

She thought tears were forming at the back of his eyes. There was always the possibility that such people might be unhinged.

'I mean, who else is there now who can say they worked with Marie Lloyd … Kate Carney … Fred Barnes? And Belle Elmore. I mean, that's an amazing thing to have in your history. If I'm not mistaken, you were on the bill at the Camberwell Empire with her, weren't you? I mean, Belle Elmore! You'd just married your second husband, I think.'

'Belle Elmore?'

Hattie was suddenly aware of the need to be elsewhere, anywhere elsewhere. Her legs unsteadied. Standing as she was, a danger to traffic and to self-preservation, in the middle of the street, listening to a sort of madman. There was a sudden need for a sight of the sea, a re-focusing. It was only just around the corner, after all. She could hear the waves making themselves known. A few minutes more and she'd be striding along the pier, heading for the safety of her dressing-room. The closing of the door against the world that carried on forever changing.

'Oh, yes. Belle Elmore! Who'd believe it, eh? You worked with her on several bills,' he said, and there was no doubting this walking encyclopaedic account of her past; if he said she had, she must have. 'She was much lower, of course, much less of a performer than you. Wines and spirits as they used to say, obviously, but I mean, you worked with her, you *knew* her. How many people can say that?'

'Yes. Of course, it's a very long time ago. I must be going. You must excuse me.'

'Of course. Lovely to have met you at last.' He stood stock still, paused, gazed deep into her eyes with the sense of wonder akin to that expressed by Howard Carter on discovering Tutankhamun. 'I so look forward to seeing you later!'

Hattie had already turned away, but switched back to face him.

'Later?'

'I couldn't let such a rare opportunity go by. I've booked for the two weeks of shows, matinees included. The same seat, third row centre aisle.'

II

At the band call, Glynis decided to get the support acts dealt with first. Hattie Prince refused to rehearse with any other artists present; Gary Rage refused to rehearse. Monty had wanted a small band in the pit but the lack of funds had meant hiring a church organist who'd just completed a successful summer season at the local crematorium. Francis christened him 'La Crème de la Crème'. He and Gordon sat in the stalls, fascinated by what was unfolding before them.

Peregrine Grenville and Elsie Balls started the proceedings, going through their selections from *Chu Chin Chow*, extracting what little comedy could be drawn from Elsie's deep bass rendition of 'The Cobbler's Song', Peregrine accompanying her with a hammer, before going into a selection from *Oklahoma!*, in which they hoped to create the illusion that Elsie's wheelchair was a surrey with a fringe on top. The wheels had a tendency to stick at crucial moments, so that Elsie had her back to the audience as she sang 'Many A New Day', but these were minor hitches that Glynis knew could be ironed out. To finish their routine the duettists threw their stetsons in the air with a last wild cry of 'Oklahoma!'

Dorothy Driscoll followed, apologising to La Crème for the state of her sheet music, last used twenty years ago at a Masonic ladies' evening in Woolwich. Her voice was not unpleasant. It had a plaintive strain, as if something elemental had once happened to her and left its mark. Bert Ambrose had arranged her music, she told them, for an act she'd done many times at Lyons Corner House in Charing Cross. 'It goes with a swing' Dorothy told La Crème, who hadn't the necessary skills, Broadway rhythm not being much in demand at cremations, but he struggled on. Francis liked Dorothy immediately, the little suggestions of sadness she put into the songs when least expected, her inability to express a convincing happiness. Gordon thought she looked the sort of woman he'd like to have as an aunt.

Parliamentary Pete was the show's comedian, with every indication that he was supremely unamusing.

'No need to go through the whole act, darling,' said Glynis, not wanting to tire him unnecessarily. He limped from the wings, peering out short-sightedly into the dark. 'If you'll just give us a taster, that would be great. You've got some music?'

'That's right. I've handed it to the gentleman of the pit. Shall we go through it? I come on after four bars.'

'The Marquis of Queensberry, the Bunch of Grapes, the Rose and Crown and the Fisherman's Retreat,' whispered Gordon.

'I'm ready when you are.'

He limped into the prompt-side wings as La Crème struck up Parliamentary Pete's entrance music, popping back almost at once with his opening song.

Pete! Pete! I'm Parliamentary Pete
I'm always sitting in the House
To rest my weary feet
Pete! Pete! Passing every law!
A blow out in the members' room
And home each day by four!

He negotiated a few shuffled steps as the little tune whimpered to its close, before beginning his comedy. Francis had to admit it: the man had a unique act, consisting of jokes about British Prime Ministers, one about the Right Honourable Charles Grey, three years in post from 1830, better known as Earl Grey (the punchline involved a cup of tea), and a joke about Lord Palmerston getting confused with parmesan after being called a big cheese.

'Haven't you anything more recent?' asked Glynis. 'Or funnier', she might have added.

Parliamentary Pete beamed back at her.

'And there's my impersonations' he said. 'I do Archibald Primrose, appointed Prime Minister 1894, Benjamin Disraeli appointed Prime Minister 1874, and William Pitt, both younger and older. They always go well.'

'But no one knows what they sounded like,' said Gordon, which was exactly what Glynis was thinking.

Heron Makepeace was next. Francis thought him a most unappealing person, still wrapped in the tight bursting-out outfit he had worn for Mrs Freebody's sherry party, his small, florid face, his tiny, florid eyes with the pinprick pupils, and the voice that had said 'Get out of the way, sonny' to Gordon in the dressing-room corridor. Now, he was handing his music over to La Crème.

'When you're ready, Heron,' said Glynis.

Giggling, spasms of which had too often marred his adolescence, remained a problem for Gordon. Francis' usual weapon against it was a sharp nudge in his cousin's ribs, but this fit was contagious. Heron Makepeace had steadied himself centre stage, as if he were a sentry rooted in his box, and, four square to the auditorium, began to sing, a sort of oily bellow, now and again moving his body a little to the left and then, a little later, to the right, before returning stiff as a rock to his post, his face immobile throughout. He was half way through, and Gordon had tightened every muscle to stifle the appalling laughter that threatened to burst out of him, when Glynis walked up to the edge of the stage and addressed the singer across the footlights. Heron was going on about someone called Rose at the time.

'Heron, love. Sorry, Heron. Nice number and everything,' said Glynis, 'but it goes on a bit, doesn't it. Know what I mean?'

'Goes on a bit?' Heron said. The speaking voice was just as oily, with an added squeak to it, as if rats were scratching at a door. 'How do you mean?'

'This is your first half spot, yes?'

'Correct.'

'It's the seven minute slot, Heron.'

'So? I don't see where this is going.'

'Nice song, but … Nothing wrong with some olde worlde charm, but …'

'Olde world charm? It's Ivor Novello!'

'Don't get me wrong. Decent number.'

'Of course it's a decent number. "Rose of England", one of Ivor's best.'

'Couldn't you make it "Rose of Cromer", I mean there's bound to be a Rose or two in the audience. You can use it to your advantage.'

'The rose in question,' said Heron, 'is horticultural, not to say symbolical, and of considerable patriotic significance.'

'Blimey. Don't get me wrong, love. I like it, keep it in, they'll lap it up, and it's a novel start.'

'I'm not writing a novel,' said Heron. 'And what do you mean, "it's a novel start"?'

'No, it's a nice touch. They won't be expecting it.'

'Why shouldn't they expect it? How would they know what to expect? I've only just come on.' His face was changing colour.

'Like I say, a clever opener. It's just, I mean I reckon you were three minutes into the song and you haven't started moving.'

'What? What do you mean, moving?'

'Three minutes more or less, and you haven't done anything but sing.'

'Are you publicly attempting to humiliate me?' asked Heron. 'I moved.'

He looked beyond her to his fellow performers dotted about in the dusk of the auditorium, as if expecting a tidal wave of sympathy.

'Will someone vouch for me? Unless I am sorely mistaken I changed position several times. Once on "who loved thee of old" – I always take two steps stage right at that moment, and then cross stage left when I get to the middle eight ...'

'No, Heron. Lovely, like I say, but not what they've paid for, is it? Where's the boa?'

'What?'

'I understood you started the act with the boa around your neck.'

'What? What on earth are you going on about? I am sorry to disappoint you, but I am not a drag act.'

'What? I wasn't suggesting you were. Just wondering when the snake comes in? Is he in the dressing-room.'

'*What*? What snake? I don't understand a thing you're saying. I'm doing the Ivor Novello numbers, with the moves as originally taught personally to me by no less than Ivor Novello himself. Man to man. I was just getting to the reverse turn anticipating the final top note, and there needs to be a follow spot, by the way, pencil definition brought on the face as I reach my climax. At no time does this involve my wearing a feather boa or going to fetch a reptile from my dressing-room.'

'Oh, I see.' Glynis smiled understandingly. 'No, not a *feather* boa, Heron. I see how we've got crossed lines. I meant the Gaboon Viper.'

'What?'

'As advertised: the Gaboon Viper. Well, any of the anaconda family, really, I don't suppose anyone will notice the difference so long as it looks poisonous. Anything long, fat and slippery round your neck will do nicely. Heron, we really have to press on with this. Can we go back a bit? It's just a case of starting the moves earlier.'

'I can't see the point of moving about before I have a reason for moving about. Ivor knew what he was doing. I have some high notes early on. It would be sheer folly to move about during those. I mean, I've already been moving as I walked on. I think that can accurately be described as movement.'

'Nice as the singing is, Heron, they've come to see your body.'

'What?'

'That's the nub of it.'

'I haven't the least idea what you're talking about. *What's* the nub of it?'

'They want to see the unique things you can do with your body. Your legs behind your neck, putting your head between your knees while bending over with your back to the auditorium, with the Gaboon Viper still in place. A fang or two might not come amiss, either. And I'm not sure "Rose of England" is going to work once you're in your leotard. I mean, I can see how striking it would be, but …'

A gurgling splutter came from where Gordon was sitting.

'I'm perfectly happy for you to do your stuff at the same time as singing "Rose of England" but as it is you've only left about four minutes left to show them you can twist and turn your body in ways that would make an ordinary person's eyes water.'

Heads turned as Gordon, a handkerchief pressed to his mouth, hurried from the auditorium. It took a few minutes more for Glynis to work out that Monty had mistakenly booked Heron Makepeace, baritone, having meant to book Harold Makepiece, contortionist.

It was left to Francis to see him back to his dressing-room. It was only later, after Heron had gone, that Francis found a scrap of paper that must have fallen to the floor from one of Makepeace's pockets.

'What do you make of this?' he asked Gordon.

'Lawks. It's a bit spooky if you ask me.'

The words looked as if they had been scrawled in anger.

I no wot 'appened!
BEWEAR!!

'Goodness knows,' said Gordon. 'It's odd, certainly. I mean, it sounds, well, threatening, doesn't it? It's not the sort of message you'd like to receive. It makes you feel guilty, feeling that someone knows something you've done that you shouldn't have done. You might know what that something is, or you might not, so that makes it even more scary. Pretty obvious it's written by someone who isn't particularly well educated.'

'You think?'

'Sounds like a coster in a music-hall song!' said Gordon. 'Look at the spelling! Whoever wrote it can't be very bright.'

He handed the note back to Francis, who seemed lost in thought.

'So, what's worrying you?'

'The apostrophe,' said Francis.

Chapter Twelve

'Just breathe that air!'

Gordon had flung wide the windows of the bedroom he and Francis were sharing at The Old Fishergirl's Hideout, letting a minor tornado blow the pretty flowered curtains across the room, and sending that week's edition of the *Eagle* flapping chaotically against the walls. 'Can't you feel it doing you good?'

'We are in danger of being marginalised,' said Francis Jones.

'*We* – possibly,' said Gordon Jones. '*You* – never!'

'The only reason I agreed to this charade was the possibility that something interesting might come of it.'

'What sort of something?'

'An *untoward* something, something that presents us with a problem.'

'Well, we're sharing a bedroom. That's a bit of a problem in itself.'

'Don't remind me,' said Francis. 'Two weeks of this! I can't help feeling the whole thing has been a dreadful mistake.'

In a way, he was right. Mr and Mrs Jones and Gordon's guardian Uncle Billy had agreed to the boys' secondment to the seaside confident that the cousins would be staying with one of their teachers at St Basil's, and his wife. The Revd Challis had confirmed that the Brownlows were greatly looking forward to putting the boys up. After all, they had both been favourite pupils of the recently retired Mr Brownlow. It was only when Mr Brownlow opened the door to his young visitors that he realised his mistake: he had been thinking of two other, quite different, less sensational, boys. The ones he had unwittingly agreed to foster for two weeks were not the ones he would have chosen from the wide selection of pupils he had taught. The younger one seemed a nice enough lad, resplendently healthy, happily freckled, bright-eyed. The older seemed well ahead of his years, a little supercilious, a little too clever-me-lad for Mr Brownlow's unimaginative taste. Of course, he knew of these boys' reputations as amateur detectives, and had heard and read of several of their adventures, no doubt exaggerated by the press. This only added to his apprehension of what the fortnight's visit would bring. To his relief, Mrs Brownlow, the eminently sensible daughter of an eminently scrupulous bishop, was the sort of woman who would have made a man-eating shark feel at home had one washed up at her front door, and a woman used to taking things out of her husband's hands without him being aware of the loss.

'Well, we may as well make the most of it,' said Gordon, who was determined to do just that. 'We can go shrimping tonight, walk the pier, case the joint.'

Shrimping! The very mention of Cromer always seemed to raise up marine life. Crabs, of course, and lifeboats. For anyone on the lookout for mystery there was no denying that Cromer was distinctly fishy. It was Francis' first visit. Gordon had often been, 'of a Sunday' as Uncle Billy said, sedately motored down from Strutton-by-the-Way. Billy's affinity with the sea made these trips so special, his delight obvious as his

Austin 7 began its slow downhill tumble into the beginning of the town, the sea, always still, spread carpet-like beyond. How often as the car slid towards its destination had Billy wound down his window and sucked in the air, as noisily as if he was the thirstiest mariner alive, breaking into a hymn of sorts as inch by inch the town crept closer.

'Oh, where is the land of I dunno where? Dreamy the driver who takes you there. Climb in his car and away you start, and he won't charge much for the fare.'

Gordon was joining in by then.

'When you get to the land of I dunno where, don't be surprised at the wonders there' and they la-la'd a line neither of them was sure of, and 'a pig can't fly' and then, the big in unison finish 'Where? I dunno know where!'

Billy would wind the window down further and swerve slightly.

'Can you hear it, lad?' he'd ask, 'can you hear the bells? You will! You will!', and then he'd tell about the times of one of the King Henrys and how an old settlement had been lost in the sea, and how its bells still tolled out of the deep for those who wanted to hear them, and Gordon would listen hard and take in rejuvenating gusts of the wild, heather-peppered hills that had withstood centuries across the top of the town.

Charming as their temporary bedroom at the top of the Old Fishergirl's Hideout was, Francis felt constrained by the slanting roof, as if at any moment he might meet someone from *Alice in Wonderland*. He bumped his head on one of the beams. Come to think of it, a stroll along the prom, prom, prom might be preferable. All the girls were lovely by the seaside, after all! Oh the seaside girls! All the girls are lovely by the sea, their curls and bits of drapery! The ocean! What a commotion! Come along where the breezes blow, off to the briny we must go! They're all lovely by the sea!

Try as he might, Francis found it hard not to be drawn in. The image of his mother loosening a corset couldn't be avoided. Something was, what was that word? … *giving*. Whatever it was, he knew it was meant to be, this is how the markings of your life were made. Just when he thought it pointed one way, it pointed another, pointed to somewhere off the track, down a lane, around a corner.

There had been signs. A few weeks earlier, he'd heard on the Third Programme a piece about music-hall. The first thing he'd learned was how it was hyphenated, so that whatever sort of music was involved was somehow defined, kept apart. Extracts from some ancient acoustic recordings had been played, the sound so feeble that he had to hug the wireless close to catch some of the words. The first voice he heard was Victoria Monks, who had once celebrated sweet Saturday night, when your week's work is over, because that's the evening you make a throng, take your dear little girl along. That wasn't what they were playing on the wireless, and they'd only mentioned her best known 'Bill Bailey Won't You Please Come Home?', a song that Francis hated when he'd heard it bawled out somewhere. Instead, they played one of Victoria Monks' most haunting songs, 'Movin' Day'.

It had the stamp of personal tragedy about it – not the sort of tragedy that Shakespeare would have bothered with – but the tragedy of the little man, the unimportant, the man in the street, the person who went to his grave wondering what everything that had happened in life had been about. The song, the voice, the tangible contact with a world so long vanished, caught Francis unexpectedly, sparked something in him that he knew would lead on to something else, somewhere – maybe the land of I dunno where, the land that Uncle Billy sang of to Gordon every time they motored down the hill into Cromer. Of course, Francis had heard music-hall songs before, outside pubs at closing time or early doors. He'd heard Florrie Forde chorusing Antonio and his ice cream cart, asking a naughty boy to hold out his hand, and the sickening call to alms dressed up in the clattering rhythm of 'It's A Long Way To Tipperary', but until that moment he had never guessed what a passion those old songs would wake in him.

He couldn't get Victoria Monks' voice out of his head. One of the lesser known performers on the music-halls, she'd recorded 'Give My Regards To Leicester Square' in 1905. When she died, Walter Sickert wrote to *The Times*, reminding its readers that 'while the great literary poets have been able to achieve the same results for eternity, the coincidence of the writer, the composer and the singer, is only engraved in the frail hearts and the frailer brains of the disappearing generations'. No less than T S Eliot (Francis had tried reading *Four Quartets* and failed, shamefacedly returning to Agatha Christie's *Hickory Dickory Dock*) had lamented the passing of Marie Lloyd, insisting that 'no other comedian succeeded so well in giving expression to the life of that audience, in raising it to a kind of art. It was, I think, this capacity for expressing the soul of the people that made Marie Lloyd unique and that made her audiences, even when they joined in the chorus, not so much hilarious as happy.' Eliot's phrase had struck Francis like a thunderbolt. Something that made people feel 'not so much hilarious as happy' was surely worth hanging on to.

Yet, there was nothing remotely happy, not a hint of hilarity, in 'Movin' Day' or the way Victoria Monks (Francis had never heard of her before – Marie Lloyd and his father's favourite Harry Champion marked his boundaries) sang it. No, Francis thought. Not sang it – *communicated* it, passed it on.

Perhaps being in Cromer on geriatric manoeuvres wasn't such a bad thing after all. Only a few weeks after hearing Victoria Monks, here he was among a few of whom were left of the music-halls. There was little hope of learning anymore about it at Branlingham Branch Library, and there was nothing on the shelves, but sitting behind the counter with a Wagon Wheel at hand was the Rhonddha Valley's most well-read export to East Anglia, Blodwyn Williams, a Welsh Fountain of Knowledge.

'Francis! You're the last person I'd imagine would be interested in that old stuff.'

'I don't know that I *am* interested,' he said defensively. 'I know nothing about it. Does it matter?'

'Well, I know I'm from the valleys and all that, but oh yes, oh yes, it matters. It's history, that's what, and not dry old history, a history of fun and anquish and how things were.'

'As a matter of fact,' said Francis, and told her how he and Gordon were being deported to Cromer to help the aged performers up and down the pier.

'That's marvellous!' cried Blodwyn. 'Oh Francis, I'd be so excited in your shoes. I read about the show in the paper. Hattie Prince, no less.'

'Who?'

'You wait and see. A star, I mean a real star, not like these fly-by-nights nowadays, these here today and gone tomorrows. You couldn't have a greater name. I mean, she was never the most famous, but it's the end of the line, see, and she's one of the very last, and it's an art that's disappeared. Male impersonation. Funny, that, how female impersonation's still on the go, but male impersonation's a thing of the past ... now that's a mystery you and Gordon can solve for a start!'

'Well,' said Francis, beginning to doubt his interest, 'I'm not sure there's any point in it.'

Blodwyn snapped off a segment of her Wagon Wheel for future consumption.

'Go on! I know you, Francis. Look at it this way. What a perfect reason for getting in touch with such a past. I know I'm from the valleys and all that, but what I wouldn't give to be there. Who else is on the bill?'

'I've no idea, really, except a pop singer, but it's the oldies we'll be helping with.'

'How d'you mean? Backstage?'

'I think Mr Challis was thinking of us more as helping hands, there for the elderly when needed. Cups of tea, helping them up and down the pier, going on errands, words of encouragement, handing out medication. Little cousins of mercy, really.'

He tried to sound enthusiastic, although the prospect of being at the beck and call of a crowd of hardened old theatricals was already flashing up warnings. But if the Brownlows came up trumps, he and Gordon would have most of the days (except matinee days) to themselves, and if the weather stayed fine, there was the beach and the cliffs. Hadn't someone written a parlour song 'A Perfect Day', inspired by the cliffs of Cromer or thereabouts, to be sung around the piano? There was a fine parish church, the sort of location that M R James (Francis was currently devouring his *Tales of an Antiquary*) might have used for a horror story, and the sort of place that Francis – with vague inclinations to being an antiquarian manqué – felt he should visit, and Poppyland, a fashionable watering place along the coast around Overstrand, where another of Francis' favourites, E F Benson, had golfed each summer. Come to think of it, the whole thing might work out well, especially if their ghosts were about.

Blodwyn never doubted it. She was smiling, her mouth from long practice wide as one of her trademark Wagon Wheels, and kicked back her chair. Francis didn't know how to explain it, but it was as if her everyday boiler suit had inexplicably turned into something by Norman Hartnell.

'There's nothing like a holiday,' she began, 'when your knees are giving way, to make you feel like a jack-in-the-box, so shout hip hip hoorah for the good old holiday time, good old, jolly, holiday time. Thunder, lightning, rain or snow, it's holiday time and so we've got to go where the girls look bonny and prime, in their dainty twiddly bits of lime. Everywhere is like a fair, we're all devil may care, because it's holiday time!'

Francis had stood, entranced, because Blodwyn didn't stop there, but went on, announcing each of the artistes she was recreating. Daisy Dormer, the Dutch delight 'Happy' Fanny Fields singing 'By The Side Of The Zuider Zee' (fortunately, Blodwyn was wearing her usual clogs), and Marie Lloyd's 'She arrived at Euston by the midnight train, but when she got to the wicket then someone wanted to punch her ticket' and, her boiler suit now standing in for a tea-gown, 'When I Take My Morning Promenade' and he couldn't remember what else. The embarrassment of Blodwyn careering around the library and throwing her head back in song as if she was second turn at the Old Metropolitan was keenly felt by those in search of literary sustenance (Miss Simms, the postmistress, had arrived in high hopes of the latest Violet Winspear romantic novel, preferably populated by a swarthy sheikh conjured up by Violet who lived in a bungalow), but Francis – much to his surprise – relaxed at once.

Blodwyn worked herself into a frenzy, pausing now and then to hand over a book or take an overdue fine (Miss Simms argued about the accuracy of the rubber stampings but handed over tuppence), managing a grand finale with Alice Lloyd's 'The Nearer The Bone, The Sweeter The Meat'. Retreating to the vestibule of the library, Miss Simms made a note of the vulgar phrase in her pocket book. What an exhibition! She would convey the conduct of Blodwyn Williams, and the off-colour lyric she had screeched out to all and sundry, to the local council. On the rates, too! She had always regarded the music-hall as the lowest form of entertainment. She deeply regretted the fact that so many of the words and tunes of those dreadful old songs had long ago wormed their way into her head, where they stubbornly remained.

CHAPTER THIRTEEN

A magnificent autumnal sunset spread itself for Cromer's delight on the opening night of *Forget-Me-Not*. The sense of anticipated pleasure, enhanced by the extraordinary quality of evening light after an afternoon of heavy rain, ran virus-like through the crowds. At such moments, the little town itself faded into a background of everyday, dull and looming above the landscape that only God himself could have provided. The sea, at its angriest when shopkeepers had put up their shutters at the end of a busy day of trading, had resolved into a calm, unfathomable blue-black, above it a blood orange sun intent on its slow collapse into the deep.

Outside the pier, those who had only just learned of that evening's event and those who had been unlucky in securing a ticket to view the spectacle, hovered, vaguely aware that something special might be happening. Unknown to them, the artistes that would be performing had long ago settled themselves in their dressing-rooms. Gary Rage had escaped the attention of all but two young women who had penetrated his disguise (sunglasses and an upturned coat collar) as he walked the pier. Hattie Prince had arrived, unrecognised, four hours earlier.

The first excitement offered on the forecourt immediately prior to the performance was the arrival of local dignitaries.

The Chairman of the Cromer Urban District Council, distinguishable merely from the official car in which he arrived and the chain (in need of Brasso) he wore around his neck, drew some interest. The highlight was the appearance of the gleaming Rolls Royce that Lady Darting's chauffer Dimple steered with funereal slowness down the slope to the edge of the pier's entrance. He pulled the vehicle to an aristocratic standstill and emerged, perfectly suited, his peaked cap and stern expression emphasising the importance of the parcel he was delivering, opening the rear passenger door with remarkable authority as if unveiling something of unquestionable quality.

Lady Darting emerged, followed a moment or two later by Lady Cynthia, who for the rest of the evening remained, rather in the style of the Duke of Edinburgh, two steps behind Lady Darting. The dignitaries had lined up in a welcoming committee at the entrance to the pier. The Chairman of the Cromer Urban District Council's wife, having only a loose idea of etiquette, had gone into a deep curtsey as soon as Lady Darting's feet touched the ground, quickly realising that she would very soon have to do it all over again when her ladyship reached her in the queue. Trained to deal with any social indiscretion, the evening's most high-born guest of honour pretended not to have noticed.

Lady Darting was wearing an enormous boa made from the plumage of an Abyssinian skylark shot by her Uncle Remus (an event that had marked the total extinction of the breed), a cape composed of several moles (willed to her by an old gamekeeper), a headpiece of ostrich feathers, a snakeskin blouse, and a handbag kindly donated by a not unfriendly crocodile that her Great Aunt Beatrice Darting (OBE) had shot up the Impopo in 1873. Francis had come out of the theatre to catch the arrival of the local dignitaries. He had not expected the arrival of a portable zoo.

By an accident of timing, Mr and Mrs Jones showed up at the very moment Lady Darting strode forward to shake the hands of the committee. The crowd's applause that greeted her ladyship's arrival turned Mrs Jones' head. Well-known as she was in Branlingham for her pastry-making, inventive corsetry and roles in grand opera, Mrs Jones had not realised how appreciated she was in Cromer. Francis made himself as invisible as possible as his mother somehow fell in line behind Lady Darting along the line of dignitaries, shaking each by the hand. Further muddled by this, the wife of the Chairman gave Mrs Jones an even deeper curtsey than she had given Lady Darting, and almost toppled into the arms of the local Chief Constable. In her way, Mrs Jones was quite as impressive as Branlingham's *grande dame*. Held together by hosiery of her own design, she was vividly presented in a dress smothered with scarlet poppies. When she curtsied, it gave the impression that she was sitting in a field of them. Her husband had dug deep in the wardrobe at Red Cherry House to rediscover the ten-shilling suit he had worn at his wedding and that he subsequently wore on equally dubious occasions.

Glynis hovered backstage, having telephoned Monty that everything seemed to be going as well as could be expected. Yes, she'd sorted out the Heron Makepeace problem, yes Gary-stroke-Harry had been happy to mix his pop stuff with some of the music-hall stuff, that Elsie had been the trickiest to get on with, that Francis and Gordon were godsends, that Hattie had so far behaved herself, at the same time as maintaining an hauteur that kept her aloof from the others, and that it was a case of fingers crossed when it came to the organist. Happily, a port and lemon helped La Crème relax. Glynis hoped he would loosen up as the evening progressed. Not being a regular drinker, the port and lemon went straight to his head. When his fingers touched his instrument, he let out such a volley of sound that the St John Ambulance had to be summoned to an elderly patron in the front row. Glynis knew they were in for an invigorating night.

The curtains opened to reveal a winter wonderland scene, presumably meant as an advance warning of what Cromer was headed for in the coming months, with the Cromer Lovelies dressed in skimpy Eskimo wear and tap shoes. This segued into a walk-down presentation of the show's less auspicious stars, synchronised so that by the time they were positioned in line at the front of the stage they went into 'Here We Are Again'. Technically inaccurate as this was, for none of them had previously appeared on Cromer Pier, the selection of individual items that followed promised a decent night ahead.

Henry's voice was particularly strong for an illusionist, but of course he'd started as a blacked-up coon crooner when such a phenomenon was politically acceptable. His 'Lily Of Laguna' had an easy lilt, he leaned into the song, caressing its words and stepping here and there with a sway of his body that made people wonder why he was billed as a conjuror.

Dorothy Driscoll opened her spot with 'I Was A Good Little Girl Till I Met You', reviving the mischievous twinkle of the eye that had got her noticed decades before. The temperature dropped when Heron Makepeace sang 'Thank God For A Garden', a pleasing ballad that seemed slightly inappropriate when the scenery displayed a frozen landscape. The sense of refinement was amplified by the entrance of Elsie

Balls, wheeled on from the wings by Perry. Once in position, their arrangement of 'Come To The Ball' remained stationary.

It was Len's turn next. He looked as embarrassed as the audience felt. After all, he'd never been on stage before, but Glynis had said it would be wrong to leave him out, there was always a first time, she said, although why he had to do 'I Wouldn't Leave My Little Wooden Hut For You' escaped him. Of course, she had to include Parliamentary Pete in the opening. She would have preferred to leave him in his dressing-room until he came on for his act, but she needed to fill the stage, create a sense of communal fun in a show that was basically a series of stand-alone turns. He had offered 'Boiled Beef And Carrots', which he had done for years, peppering the song with violent stamping of his feet in the hope that it would remind people of its originator Harry Champion. For obvious reasons, this display was currently inadvisable.

Then, as the company formed a shape around the edges of the stage, the Cromer Lovelies (Doreen, Georgette, and sisters Marilyn and Mary-Ann) were back. After a few strenuous moves, the four girls parted into twos, making the space through which the show's stars would enter. Glynis, now sitting at the back of the theatre, hugged her stomach and held her breath. When she'd told Monty about what she had planned for that moment he'd laughed, said it would never do, that Hattie would never agree to it, but from one side of the stage walked Gary Rage, from the other Hattie Prince. They met in the middle, shook hands and walked down centre stage to noisy acclaim.

Glynis thought this was a great theatrical moment, something akin to that Christmas Eve when German soldiers and British Tommies walked towards one another across No

Man's Land during a pause in hostilities, walked towards one another, shook hands, drank schnapps, exchanged garbled words of each other's languages. It was the meeting of two worlds, the now and then, Hattie in her male splendour, top hatted, tailed, Gary in a lamé suit, all youthfulness and quiet vigour. It had been Glynis' idea too, to have them sing 'For He's A Jolly Good Fellow' to one another, and shake hands, like in No Man's Land. Then, Hattie and Gary made a point of befriending and relaxing the audience, the rest of the company lining alongside them as they went into a chorus of 'Just Like The Ivy' before the curtain wiped them away. The applause was deafening.

The Cromer Lovelies (Doreen was by far the best dancer, having won cups) came back to welcome Heron Makepeace for his solo spot. Glynis thought it better to have him done with as soon as possible. He began with 'Three Coins In The Fountain'. In its closing moments, as he reached 'Make it soon! Make it soon! Make it soon!' he stretched on tip-toe at the approach of each top note, his dentures rattling dangerously. The same thing had happened at the bingo hall whenever he said 'Clickety-Click'. At his back, a water feature on loan from a local garden shop trickled ever more loudly, amplified by a badly placed microphone that made it sound as if he was beside Niagara Falls. To close, Heron sang 'This Is My Lovely Day', with its lyric that 'this is the day I shall remember the day I'm dying', to which his croaking vocalising added a touch of authenticity. The applause was polite.

Dorothy Driscoll picked the show up, coming on in a surge of lightness and enjoyment that reached every part of the building. She got the audience at once with a marvellous introductory speech: 'Hello, everyone! I'm Dorothy Driscoll, the Doll with the Dimple. Of course, the dimple isn't where it used to be!' Directly, she burst into 'It's A Lovely Day Today'. It was clear from the beginning what skills she had honed from years of second or third rate light entertainments, via Montmorency's Minstrels (Teignmouth, 1923), The Merry Marauders (two seasons at Morecambe, 1925 and 6), Grayston Burgess' "Evenin 'All" (she'd told Grayston the title spelt disaster for matinees) at Ayr in the 1930s. She was well set up for her ENSA work alongside Bill in their dance act during the war. She knew how to take off a hat or a glove or a shoe, how and when to sit, when to stand still and when to make the slightest of gestures, where to position each leg (something essential, for obvious reasons, for Parliamentary Pete), how to settle an audience, how to raise them from their torpor. Free as air as she seemed on her entrance, she could switch to something that would wrench at your emotions, enough to start tears pricking at the back of your eyes. She handed herself over the footlights. The pricking started as she began 'I'll Be Seeing You', when she seemed to do something with time itself, drawing from each of the spectators something never forgotten and regretted. Sometimes when she sang it, she thought of the happy days she'd spent with Harry, before he'd made off with everything.

The mood changed when she went into a medley of music-hall choruses to rouse the audience into a spate of community singing. Efficient as this was, it didn't seem to Gordon to bring out the best in her. Hers was essentially an act that traded on sadness, but she flung out the old Florrie Forde favourites, 'Hold Your Hand Out Naughty Boy' and Marie Lloyd's 'A Bit Of A Ruin That Cromwell Knocked About A Bit' and 'My Old Man'. Nevertheless, her heart had gone behind the sun, until, the lights dimming to a faint Technicolor glow behind her, she laid it bare again with 'Just Like The Ivy'. She seemed to luxuriate in its hopelessness, the cockney stretching of her consonants only making it more splendid.

Glynis had always thought magicians the most boring of performers. Amazing as their achievements were, they were merely tricks, so in theory anyone could do what they did. Now, Henry had a solo turn of eight, long, minutes, some card manipulation that emphasised the tremor in his black-veined hands, at the top of the act pulling a rabbit out of a hat that had patently been rabbit-free when first shown to the audience. Len watched anxiously from the wings. They'd been through this routine umpteen times at the digs, not always successfully. It had been twenty years since Henry had done it. Nimble fingers, that was the secret, he knew. Len sighed with relief when the ten of spades, and it really seemed as if it might be magic, was revealed by Henry as the one the audience member had requested. Only pulling the rabbit out of the hat remained and he could get Henry back to the dressing-room. A hapless woman from Happisburgh had been lured up on stage to inspect Henry's top hat. He made her peer deep into it, put it on her head, then take it off and show it to the audience to prove its total emptiness. He asked her to step aside (that was when he did the switch) and then, in tune with a crashing chord on the organ from La Crème, Henry dug his hand deep into the top hat. He struggled to get hold of one of the rabbit's ears, so it came out lopsided as if it had been put out to dry with one peg on a washing line. From where Len stood he could see its eyes were glazed. Henry bumped it about a bit to get some life going, but the eyes had already stopped looking. He stuffed it hastily back into the hat. One of its ears looped over the edge to remind everyone it was still there.

The Cromer Lovelies returned with a sense of purpose in shimmering evening gowns. Something was up! The boy I love is up in the gallery. The boy I love is looking down at me. There he is, can't you see, wavin' of his handkerchee, as merry as the robin that sings in the tree. Glynis couldn't have imagined anything less appropriate to introduce a genuinely handsome young pop-singer whose face was already becoming known on the covers of teenage magazines, on television and records. A burst of applause swept over the place as Gary Rage appeared. Oh, that quiff! Oh, that powder-blue suit, oh, that white shirt faintly revealing a hint of chest (said in the magazines to be delicate), and oh, the white winkle-pickers! Oh, that face, unlined but with the hint of character and goodness in it! He was a picture of British youth, of contained health. There was no doubt he was a good son to his mother, his teeth even and snow-white, his lush but neatly brushed hair, his long fingers now and again ploughing through it. Oh, what those fingers might do!

Even as he sang there were those that night that looked on thinking twenty, thirty, years ahead, how they would sit wrinkled and satisfied, to tell their descendants that they were there, how they had seen Gary Rage live on stage at Cromer Pier in 1957, and how that night glowed in memory. Would he sing their favourite number, the one that had got to number 25 (it had been 30 last week) in the charts? Well, he did and he didn't. Again, it had been Glynis' idea, and Gary put his head on one side doubtfully and said he didn't think so but they'd tried it out and it had worked, mixing an old song, one of those old music-hall ones that Glynis now went on and on about, with two or three of his own. The Cromer Lovelies came back as he reached the end of his act, lifting their arms heavenward, pointing in the direction to which that audience felt it had been transported.

The houselights brought the audience momentarily to its senses for the interval. The Chairman of the District rose with difficulty from the seat that had effectively wedged him into position as the rest of the spectators sat stock still. Lady Darting rose with some ceremony, her skylarks vibrating as if about to take flight in the cool breeze that was coming in through the now opened exit doors. Lady Cynthia rose a few seconds later, moving ghostlike at the Duke of Edinburgh distance from her ladyship. The party made their way along the row to the aisle, conquering several obstacles (an oversized woman with plump knees, an umbrella whose spokes nearly took out the Chairman of the Cromer Urban District's eye, and a raincoat buckle that got entangled with Lady Cynthia's reticule) to the end of the row towards the gangway, and were escorted to the bar by the theatre manager, where the more refined refreshments for the party had been laid out. Separated from the rest of the audience by a roped-off area (Lady Darting had insisted that her socialist principals would not allow her to be taken to a private room) Lady Darting was sustained with a 1924 Batard Montrachet, while Lady Cynthia smoked a pipe. No sooner had these festivities commenced than the end-of-interval bell was rung and the VIP guests made their way back to their seats, overcoming the same obstacles they had encountered on the way out but in reverse order (the raincoat buckle, the umbrella spokes and the big knees).

CHAPTER FOURTEEN

Glynis, returning for the second half to her hideaway seat at the back of the auditorium, felt the tangible sense of expectation in the air. There was no doubt to what it was directed. Monty had bombarded the local newspapers with stuff about Hattie, heavily loaded with the great risk that, at her advanced age, the old girl might never so much as make it on stage, let alone to the end of the evening, and most likely to the end of the run. Heavens! Extraordinary as it seemed, only a few days before beginning rehearsals, the woman had been in a nursing home. The matron of that establishment, a Miss Deirdre Corbett, had subsequently been interviewed by no less than *The Times*. Miss Corbett explained that it had been a privilege to care for dear Miss Prince (or dear Mrs McPhee as she had then been known), and that barring an unexpected medical blip which might yet strike her down (at her age, after all, it was a wonder that she was preparing for a twenty-five minute appearance on stage), audiences would experience something quite unique. If the blip should occur, she would be welcomed back at 'Evermore' with open arms.

It was the prospect of Hattie's epic turn at the top of the evening that set the audience a-bubble. A peak had already been achieved by Gary Rage. How could an old woman take them to that level? A sort of impatience filled the air. Whatever happened between now and Hattie's act could only be filling in, and the quicker done the better. The Cromer Lovelies restarted the proceedings with a Television Topper-like routine, high kicking synchronised horses, Dorothy joining them for 'Come On, Algernon'.

Glynis' last minute booking of Ravel and Rita performed the contortions Heron Makepeace had been unable to provide. They were Hungarian, and spoke no English. In the circumstances, everyone thought they must be husband and wife, as no other relationship would have seemed decent when their contortions forced them into such un-British positions. Their manoeuvres were accompanied by Ravel's *Bolero*, so that their initial movements, many of them eye-watering, were done at a snail's pace, until the music quickened into a furious rampage, forcing Ravel and Rita to tie themselves in knots at alarming speed.

Glynis sensed that the audience's patience was stretched to the limit when Grenville and Elsie returned. In less generous mood, now only wanting Hattie, it politely endured the elderly duettists. Perry wheeled Elsie on, singing as he pushed, 'Tell Me, Pretty Maiden, Are There Any More At Home Like You?'. With her eyes transfixed somewhere towards the spheres, Elsie concluded their brief interlude with 'I Love The Moon' while Perry posed, a pensionable Cupid only half in the off-course follow spot.

It was possible that worse was to come: Parliamentary Pete. Glynis had done the best she could with him, couldn't understand why Monty had recommended him. Glynis, as gently as she knew how, had asked the old boy not to mention his leg (which one?, he'd asked her a little rattily) or, if medically possible, not to draw attention to it, but there was nothing she could do about his appalling material. She'd cut him down to eight minutes. The silence that greeted his opening patter confirmed her suspicion that Monty had been mistaken. Her only hope now was that the Great Zultan would get the show up and going again. A few titters greeted Pete's third joke, his fourth got a few more, and so it slowly grew. In three minutes, he had the place rocking with laughter. It wasn't what he said. What he said wasn't funny, never had been and never would be. It was the way he said it. Deadpan, as if he didn't care if the audience was there or not, but Pete was listening to every clue the audience gave him, where to drop this word, place that look. To Glynis, it had seemed a ragbag of hopelessly unfunny rubbish, but after ten minutes, the roar of pleasure that lifted the roof helped him walk into the wings with no hint of a limp. From a list of dry as dust British Prime Ministers that no one under the age of a hundred might have heard of, Parliamentary Pete had fashioned brilliance.

Now, it needed only Henry and Len's spot to get the show through to Hattie. Glynis didn't know about the rabbit. Henry had nipped out of the stage door as soon as he'd come off and plopped it into the sea when no one was about. Len was furious when the rabbit didn't come back, sat in the corner of the dressing room and cried. Henry told him to pull himself together, they needed to test the boxes, make sure the doors of the cabinet didn't need oiling. So much depended on a total blackout. You wouldn't want to come back to life when you weren't supposed to be there, would you now, Henry asked, egg on your face, and of course Len had no answer, and his stomach was revolving quicker than the cabinet would be in ten minutes. And remember, for God's sake don't forget, Henry said, it's when I knock on the box *three* times that you pull the switch. *Three times*! And don't look too smug at the end, he said, when we take the bow. Remember you're an eastern slave, only there to do my bidding. Think inscrutable!

The most easternly music La Crème could come up with was 'In A Monastery Garden'. Henry was on first, of course, appearing as if from nowhere via a sort of explosion that made the audience jump out of its skin. He was impressive, too, his flowing robes, his Turkish slippers, the bangles and beads festooned around him, his features so brown that it seemed as if he'd just returned from a package tour of Arabian deserts, and magnificent eyebrows.

Len waited for his cue, and on he went. The audience applauded because Henry had indicated to them that they should. It unnerved rather than encouraged Len, but he knew what he had to do, how vital it was to follow Henry's instructions, how every second counted. Once under way, things went well. This is where they'll clap, Henry had said about this or that moment, and he'd been right every time. First time out, and Len was learning how to get an audience doing exactly what it was supposed to.

By now, La Crème was playing snake-charming music, then Henry did the getting someone up on stage stuff. It was a woman, looked as if she might work in a chemist's. If you pick the wrong one, Henry had told him, you're buggered. There's a skill to it, like shooting a tiger, you have to look them in the eyes before you drag them up on stage. At first, she seemed like the wrong one. Henry had to twice explain what he wanted her to do with the handcuffs, and Len was worried because if they went on wrong she might mess everything up and he'd get the blame likely as not. He needn't have worried, though. Henry improvised and more or less put the handcuffs on Len himself.

And so into the box. For the first time, now it was for real, Len realised how dark it was in there, black as pitch, no-moon, mole-surrounding gloom. As if from miles away, he was conscious of La Crème going like mad, pulling out all the stops or whatever you had to do on an electronic organ to make it sound like the end of the world. The thick velvet curtains that helped mystify the space Len was occupying muffled the sounds, as if the audience wasn't there, which of course it was, there and waiting for something unbelievable to happen in front of its eyes. Len panicked. In this crepuscular nothingness how was he to find the lever that would make him vanish? He fumbled. La Crème was holding on to a chord, sustaining it because he knew he should until Henry did the reveal and Len was suddenly there again. Through the curtains Len heard Henry hissing at him but couldn't make out the words.

At last, he found the lever, took a deep breath and forced it down, straight, hard down as Henry had said he must. This was the last test, when he had to straighten and twist his body into the compartment hidden from public view. And then, he reappeared, to a gasp from the audience. It was the first time in his life that Len knew people were pleased to see him. They took their bows, Henry going back again for a solo call after he'd shared one with Len. It had taken it out of the Great Zultan, his chest heaving like a grampus on his way back to the dressing room, where Len gave him a tot of whisky.

They passed Hattie, waiting in the wings. The roar that went up as she walked on stage echoed on and on. Hattie Prince, 86 years old, in her twenty-five minute spot. Francis and Gordon were in the prompt corner. They never forgot that night.

Gordon, as instructed, stood in the wings throughout, holding the handbag.

CHAPTER FIFTEEN

I

Inspector Bellairs took a long hard look at the North Sea.

It needed to be stared out, all that water. He had been transferred from London's dockland only a month before, and Norfolk was going to take some getting used to. The skies, for a start, a vast canopy over a surprisingly horizontal landscape, and on this chilly morning on the North Norfolk coast in early autumn, grey. To the little gathering of people waiting at the edge of the car park, a journalist from the local newspaper, and a reporter from the BBC, the man stepping out of the car had neither the height nor the bearing that they associated with the police force. The BBC reporter saw an unphotogenic face. Bellairs' wife had said as much more than once, but had anyway smudged it fondly before he left home this morning. A uniformed officer walked towards him from the cliff-top café.

'Good morning, sir. P C Bradshaw.'

'Morning, lad. Opened early for you, have they?'

Bellairs nodded towards the surprisingly eloquent hut that provided refreshment for cliff walkers. He hadn't had much of a breakfast.

'More for the elderly gentleman, sir.' Bradshaw indicated a bearded man with a stick and a dog sitting outside the café. 'He found the body. Nasty shock. Tea works wonders with a dab of brandy.'

'It's nippy,' said Bellairs. He could already hear the sea, far above it as he was. 'Shall we go down? What do we know?'

'Mr Gearing found the body, or rather his dog did, around eight o'clock this morning. He always starts his days early, likes to get down here for a stretch with Honolulu Lola before the holidaymakers arrive.'

As there was no gangster's moll to be seen, Bellairs' police training told him Honolulu Lola must be the old man's dog.

'Would many people make it this far? It's a bit of a stretch from the main beach.'

The young constable was leading the way down. Rough-hewn steps wound steeply from the cliff face. One of the good things about dockland was he'd never had far to walk, but three minutes after starting off along the beach, he could see they still had some way to go before reaching their destination. It was Bellairs' first time for walking on sand since he'd been a teenager, and it was heavy going. Bradshaw explained that the path they'd come down by was the safest route, more convenient approaches having been made impassable by erosion.

Getting closer, Bellairs was relieved to see Sergeant Hedgecraft hailing them across the sand. He couldn't have been matched with a more dependable officer, a solid, well set-up, calmly efficient local man with more than a dash of common sense and not too obvious ambition. As soon as Bellairs had arrived in Norfolk, Hedgecraft and he had fitted, two pieces of a jigsaw, but there was no sign of the other figure Bellairs was expecting to see.

'Morning, Dan. Inspector Slaughter not here yet?'

'No, sir. He's off the case. Super rang to tell me you'd be heading up instead. Rang you at home but you'd already left.'

'What?'

Bellairs hoped his relief wasn't too obvious. His brief experience of working alongside 'Tod' Slaughter wasn't something he wanted to repeat.

'You should be so lucky.' The woman was kneeling by the body. 'Harriet Wayworth, Chief Medical Officer. Good to meet you, Mr Bellairs. Welcome to the seaside.'

Bellairs would have shaken her hand if it hadn't been for the rubber gloves.

'Poor chap.' He looked down at the crumpled heap. 'What can you tell us?'

'A male, middle-aged. He's been dead for some time, perhaps eight or nine hours. No obvious signs of injury having been inflicted.'

'But he fell from the cliff?'

'That's probably what killed him, yes. The splay of his legs and arms suggests he floundered on the way down. Well, you would, wouldn't you? It's quite a height. I'll know more when we get the body back to the lab.'

'Identification?'

'Nothing on him,' said Hedgecraft. 'One thing, though. He's got make-up on.'

'Oh, well. Each to his own,' said Bellairs.

'Around the eyes. Mascara. Some sort of oil-based lipstick, and two carmine spots in the corner of his eyes.'

'What do you make of that?'

'The carmine spots?' Wayworth smiled up at them. 'It's an old theatrical trick. Accentuates the eyes, concentrates the mind. Basically, red greasepaint.'

'We were just saying, sir, how that might tie up,' said Hedgecraft. 'We've had a report of a missing person. He's in the show on Cromer Pier. The landlady at his digs rang the station this morning when she found his bed hadn't been slept in, but there's no identification on him. I've sent a car for the woman who's in charge of the show. Let's see if she identifies him.'

Glynis arrived five minutes later. She could see, from far off along the sand, that it was Heron, still enough of his puffy, slightly penguin shape rising above the beach.

'Yes,' she said. 'It's Heron Makepeace.'

She suddenly realised how very alone the man had seemed to her.

'I don't know about next of kin. There must be someone, I suppose. I don't know much about him at all, really. How horrible.'

'We'll sort that, miss,' said Hedgecraft. 'We can do you a cup of tea at the café, if you'd like.'

'Yes. Yes, I think it's gone to my legs. I think that might be a good idea. Thank you.'

'Thing is,' whispered Bellairs to Hedgecraft as he moved off to escort Glynis back to the cliff top, 'did he jump or was he pushed?'

Hedgecraft moved his arm lightly across Glynis' back to guide her. Fortunately, the dead man's face hadn't been visible, having embedded itself in the sand, but his arms and legs looked as if they might have been arranged for the cover illustration of a lurid detective story, the victim's body twisted this way and that, as if someone had tried to make a swastika out of him, at least making the job of the policeman whose duty it was to outline the form of the corpse in chalk a little more interesting. Not that they'd chalk on sand, of course.

What was she thinking? She didn't know where her mind was leading her, only knew that probably for the first and certainly for the last time in his life, Heron Makepeace looked every inch a contortionist.

II

The shadow of Heron Makepeace's death extended far beyond Cromer. By lunchtime that day, news of the discovery had been broadcast by the BBC, suggesting there was little truth in the theory that there was no such thing as bad publicity. Listeners turned up the wireless, drawn in by the scanty information available. Perhaps this was the beginning of an extraordinary series of deaths, a dastardly plan to exterminate forgotten performers from the long-ago days of music-hall. Cromer Pier might soon be renamed the Theatre of Death, which would almost certainly be good box office. Might the other stars of yesteryear, living out their last gasps above the unreliably gusty North Sea, be snuffed out one by one, one per night perhaps? By the end of the run, audiences might be left with a one-man or one-woman (depending on the murderer's running order) show. Of course, Heron Makepeace's death had probably been accidental. It had been a black, moonless night, although why the man had decided on a midnight stroll along so perilous a path you couldn't imagine.

A police car took Bellairs, Hedgecraft and Glynis from the site of the tragedy to Mrs Freebody's. She had barely had time to clear breakfast and dust a few ornaments before they arrived. The unamused photographic study of the departed Mr Freebody, as if appalled by the fact that his once respectable abode had become not only a refuge for theatrical vagabonds but associated with a death plastered across the front page of newspapers, stared down at the sitting-room where Bellairs and Hedgecraft had installed themselves. Facing them were Grenville and Elsie, Parliamentary Pete, Henry and Len, Dorothy Driscoll, Glynis, and Mrs Freebody, for whom her late husband seemed to reserve his most sanctimonious expression.

'Good morning, ladies and gentlemen. I'm Inspector Bellairs. This is Sergeant Hedgecraft. I'm afraid we are the bearers of bad news. As I think you already know, one of your company, Mr Heron Makepeace, did not return here after last night's performance. Mrs Freebody telephoned the station this morning when she found Mr Makepeace's bed hadn't been slept in. I'm sorry to inform you that his body has been found on Cromer beach, below the cliffs.'

Elsie Balls went into what Hedgecraft later described as a theatrical swoon, hastily restored by Perry who waved a paper napkin in her face. Parliamentary Pete's leg stiffened. Dorothy Driscoll put her hand to her neck, as if checking that a noose wasn't there. Henry and Len, neither particularly happy to be in the company of two policemen, exchanged glances.

'I'm not able to give you much more information at the moment. Until we have the medical officer's report, we won't know exactly how Mr Makepeace met his death. I appreciate that this will have come as a great shock to you. Meanwhile, if you are agreeable, I would like to take this opportunity, as you're so conveniently gathered in one place, of hearing anything you may have to say that you consider relevant to this tragic event. It is of course likely that at some point we shall want to speak to you individually.'

Heads nodded, someone mumbled assent. Dorothy fumbled at her neck, realising the pearls she thought she'd put on were still upstairs in her room. A silence that needed someone to break it had begun.

'I didn't like him,' she said.

'What?' Perry, already jammed into a corner by Elsie's wheelchair, almost jerked from his chair to face her.

'Something about him,' said Dorothy. 'I'm sorry to speak ill of the dead, but there we are. I didn't care for him, and that's all there is to it. Did any of you ever work with him before?'

Nobody spoke, but heads shook.

'I did,' she said. '1950. The *Fol-de-Rols* at Margate. Lovely show, beautifully costumed. Nice company, but Heron – I think he called himself something else then – never sort of fitted in. I mean, you'll always get people who don't, but with him, it was like he felt he was worthy of being somewhere better and looked down his nose at you. Always going on about being a close friend of Ivor Novello.'

'I think I know what you mean,' said Elsie, who had been blowing her nose into the napkin. 'Didn't you feel that way about him, Perry, at the band call?'

'Oh, that fiasco,' said Henry. 'It was hilarious, inspector. Glynis thought he was a contortionist.'

'I'm sorry?'

'We hired the wrong person,' said Glynis. 'It's complicated. I'll explain later. Basically, Monty, who put the show together, Monty thought he was signing a speciality act, but it wasn't the right one. There was another Makepeace, a Harold instead of a Heron. It was a silly muddle.'

'Well, he ended up tying himself in knots at the band call, even if he wasn't a contortionist,' said Henry. 'And disrespectful as it may sound, my old mum taught me that honesty was the best policy. Let's face it, he was a god-awful singer.'

'That's what we thought in the *Fol-de-Rols*,' said Dorothy.

'To hear him sing "Rose Of England". It was a travesty,' said Elsie, getting into her stride. 'Perry and I have been doing those Novello numbers all our careers. They need style. And he had B. O., something shocking, and dentures that circled. His dental plate was completely out of control. It practically revolved when he started singing. And his vibrato ...'

Bellairs was confused. Some of this might as well have been in a foreign language.

'In a company such as this,' said Elsie, graciously seeming to ally herself with the rest of the performers, 'he was a fish out of water. You couldn't regard him as a pro, inspector.'

'What about you, lad? Leonard, is it?'

'Len, yeah. Well, I don't know. He seemed a bit sad to me. You know, a sad bloke. It hung about him, that feeling of sadness.'

'Even thinking about his breath turns my stomach,' said Elsie. 'Once you get someone else's B. O. in your nostrils ...'

'And Len's a good judge of character,' said Henry.

'We're all pros,' said Elsie, breathing deeply of Mrs Freebody's air and determined to bring them together as an entity. 'We know ourselves, and the sort of people we are. And he wasn't.'

'He showed no interest,' said Parliamentary Pete.

'You're Parliamentary Pete, I think, sir?' asked Hedgecraft.

'Proud to be so. Like I said, he showed no interest when I told him about my condition.'

Hedgecraft lifted an eyebrow.

'Having recently undergone the amputation of a leg, sergeant, but nevertheless carrying on with a career that has spanned fifty years, I explained the situation to him, and the excruciating pain I've endured, but he showed not one iota of interest.'

'Just as well he never worked with Sarah Bernhardt,' said Henry.

'We care deeply about our fellow artistes,' said Elsie. Perry momentarily looked aghast. It was the first he'd heard of it.

'It would be helpful if we could establish when Mr Makepeace was last seen,' said Bellairs, hoping to steer the conversation away from backstage twaddle. 'Perhaps if I hear from each of you in turn. Mr, Perry, is it?'

'Peregrine Grenville, yes. Well, it was last night. Only a few hours before the poor man died, probably. He was just going into his dressing room.'

'What time would that have been, sir?' asked Hedgecraft, who had brought out his notebook.

'It was just after the first half finished, around 8.30 I suppose. He had the dressing room next to Elsie and I. That was the last time I saw him. He wasn't at the walk-down.'

'The walk-down?' asked Bellairs, who hadn't any experience of theatrical lore.

'The final bows, sir,' said Hedgecraft, 'when all the company come back on stage.'

'Of course. And Mr Makepeace didn't appear?'

'No,' said Perry. 'We take the bow after him, but when he didn't show up in the wings, I wheeled Elsie on early. We just missed him out. He wasn't in the second half of the show, so for all I know he might just have got fed up and come back here rather than hang about for another hour at the theatre.'

'Unheard of!' announced Elsie, as if nailing another nail into the professional coffin of Heron Makepeace. 'Not there for the curtain call! You'd expect it of amateurs! Catch Johnny Gielgud going home half way through *Hamlet* …'

'Mr Peregrine …'

'I'm Mr Grenville, technically.'

'Right,' said Bellairs. 'Do any of you recall seeing Mr Makepeace after Mr Grenville saw him going into his dressing room at the end of the interval?'

Nobody did. Of course, they'd wondered at his not turning up for the walk-down, and Glynis had made up her mind to tackle him about such bad behaviour, and on a charity night in aid of the fire brigade too. For all anyone knew, or cared, Heron Makepeace had simply vanished, never to be seen alive again.

Mrs Freebody sat tight-lipped. What a self-obsessed lot they were. One of them might at least have raised the question of how she was going to be paid for the use of the wretched man's room.

CHAPTER SIXTEEN

I

'May?'

'Who's that?'

'What d'you mean, who's that? Who'd you think it was?'

'Peter? People think I've been widowed. I keep making excuses.'

'Daft cow.'

'Where are you phoning from?'

'Digs. Lady Macbeth's away out shopping for cut-price streaky for tomorrow's breakfast. Phones in the hall, doing nothing. Cheaper than finding a box.'

'How's it been, then?'

'How's what been?'

'You know. How is it?'

'How's what?'

'I don't like to say, Peter. You know … Your leg. How's it been?'

'Which leg?'

'THE leg.'

'If the leg I think you're referring to is the one I think you're referring to, it still isn't there. Not much of a conversation piece, is it?'

'You're all right, then? I can't stop long, love. I've got a dinner for one in the oven and the timing's tricky. How's the show going?'

'Ah. Now you're talking. You won't believe it, May.'

'Try me. I've believed everything you've told me past forty three years.'

'They laughed.'

'Yer what?'

'They laughed. They laugh every night. I've never had such applause. Tore the place up again yesterday. They've been roaring their heads off.'

'That'll be the limp, love.'

'You what?'

'Don't deceive yourself, love. It's the limp getting the laughs. A case of medical embarrassment. They feel uncomfortable seeing you in that state. Identifying you as someone on the borderline of total immobility, they let rip out of kindness.'

'What the hell are you on about? I haven't limped once. Glynis said I wasn't to. No, the act's gone well, I mean I've never had a time like it. Monty's already offered me a summer season next year. I tell you, they're bloody wetting the seats. I haven't limped once, honest injun. To be truthful, when I get on there I forget which leg is the one you've been on about.'

'Well, as long as you remember which one to take off when you get to bed.'

'It's bloody impossible having a sensible conversation with you. Aren't you pleased for me, then? I thought you'd be pleased for me.'

'Course I am, love. I'm coming down next week, Saturday, so we can come back together. Will you be phoning again?'

'I might. If I can be sure of a better reception.'

'Don't be like that, love. You mean they really laughed, like, splitting their sides laughing?'

'You'd better believe it. Must go, love. Enjoy your dinner.'

'It's got sprouts included and rich beef gravy. Says so on the packet. Where are you off to now, then?'

'We've got a show at three. Going upstairs for a kip. If you're not keen on another call I've got this number Madame Fifi gave me the night of the 1918 armistice in France.'

'She'll be sitting by the phone waiting for a call. Oh, just noticed on the packet, it's got parsnips as well.'

'Are you even listening to me?'

'Of course I am. This Fifi. She sounds right up your street.'

'She was.'

'If she's got any sense she'll have changed her number years ago.'

'Bye, love.'

'Love you, Peter. Always will. That's all that matters. It's good they're laughing, love, but what the hell if they didn't, eh? None of it matters in the end, so long as you've got home to come back to. None of it matters really, does it?'

II

The letter was waiting for Len in the dressing room he and Henry shared.

'Try Cromer Pier' was scrawled in blue by the side of the crossed-out New Clarendon Hotel, Brighton. The envelope was blue, too, Basildon Bond, and the letter on lined paper torn from a pad.

Dear Leonard

I hope you won't mind me writing to you like this. It's such a long time now that I've been wanting to. A friend of Jimmy's said he'd heard you were living in Brighton but he didn't know where. Then someone said they thought you worked at the Clarendon Hotel there, so I am hoping this might reach you.

As you can see, we are still here at Rossall in the same house. The people next door (do you remember them?) have had it updated, and it looks really nice, but you would still recognise our house. Nothing much has changed, although my husband (Keith) died three years ago. He was always going to redecorate and alter the kitchen but he got ill and never got round to it. He was taken with pneumonia but we got him home in time, so he ended his days where he wanted to be.

Jimmy said I should write. I've been thinking about doing it for a long time and he said if you don't do it now mum you never will.

It's hard to put down what I want to say. It's such a long time ago since you lived with us, and I don't know what has happened to you all these years, but I have thought of you. Always I thought of you, but even more so recently, what with one thing and another.

I want you to know how sorry I am for you going back. When Jimmy was born, it was hard, and I suppose things got on top of me so I couldn't cope. The day you had to go back was awful. I cried then and I've cried a lot since. We should never have let you go.

Please do believe me now. I still feel bad about you going back like you had to.

I have always had happy memories of when you were here, and I hope you have some as well, Leonard.

Do you remember how you used to play on the beach, and how we had that game every night, when I used to call you in like one of those boats you hire out? I used to love watching you come back from the sea – I can still see that after all this time. I've got lots of photographs of you and we get the album out and look at them. You were a nice looking boy then and I'm sure you still are.

It seems funny that Jimmy was so young when you left. He lives around the corner from here. He works in Betts' warehouse in Fleetwood. He says we did him out of a brother when you went, but like I say it was hard for us, and then Sally was born and that was the last straw, I suppose.

Someone else who remembers you was talking about you the other day. Do you remember Leonard, Mr and Mrs Spruce's son, next door? We used to get into a muddle, with you boys having the same name. He remembers you, how you used to go over the wall into the scrub along the way. He said if I was to write to send his best. He lives the other side of Blackpool, and comes back to see his parents, both still living next door.

I hope this finds you well, because we wanted to let you know you have never been forgotten. I won't forget. I have put a self-addressed and stamped envelope in with this so you can write back if you would like.

I will leave it up to you.

I just wanted you to know that if you want to you will always be welcome here.

Helen Grantley (Mrs)

Len folded the letter carefully along the printed lines of its paper, wanting to keep it neat, aligned.

III

It was only natural that Father Brennan should be a frequent visitor at St Gertrude's, although Glynis' dad would come back from the public house down by O'Cleary's smallholding with reports of loud laughter and disrespectful comments made by its regular drinkers, how nuns and priests couldn't be trusted, how they could read all about it in Chaucer said one of the drinkers who was a professor in English literature so had to be taken notice of.

Her dad never came back from the Four Bells with the smell of strong drink on him. When he spoke of how he'd passed the time he'd describe the taste of tonic water and a cup of barley wine, small in measure. He gave the impression, or seemed to give it, that he was no more than an unconcerned observer, cold sober while all around him obscenities rang out, as events of *Canterbury Tales* proportions were related.

As the only priest for miles around, it was inevitable that Father Brennan would feature in these scandals if a priest should be involved. With no name attached to the fictional priest, it would be Father Brennan's face that first came to mind, and so, with little evidence against him,

Father Brennan accumulated a reputation. If evidence was needed, it resided in the fact that he had a car, and drove it, an old car that he had bought from Murray's Garage in Killarney because he liked the colour of it (buff brown) and Murray had convinced him he was getting money off, and a car meant a priest could get from A to B and no questions asked, and much more convenient than a pushbike. Cars had back seats, for a start, made for philandering, and this was in part why Father Brennan's social life was rumoured to be Chaucerian.

There was only the one road up to St Gertrude's, for motor traffic or pedestrians, looping round from the Riley farm and up the hill where the nuns had settled, so it was only natural that Father Brennan should be driving that way and see ahead of him Glynis walking. The car smelled of leather, the vehicle a good one in its day and kept clean still, its windows spotless, and making a purring noise that set it apart from whatever surroundings it found itself in. Father Brennan managed the gears quietly, with a sense of enjoyment, the driver's window down a little and Glynis's, if she so wished, drawn down a little too. The weather was always good when he drove up behind her, she not looking round because it might be another, different, car and a different driver, and men, as her mother told her, must be guarded against.

'You'll not be coming to church so often, Glynis? There's an empty seat,' Father Brennan said. It was a reprimand, really, couched in godliness.

Well, there were reasons, said Glynis, trying to think of some or even one, even if made-up.

'Dad's got no one to help him, Father, not since Pat got the job at Dingle, and there's just so much mother can do.'

'Your dad'll miss Pat. Still, you know where we are if you want us,' said Father Brennan, and Glynis was left wondering who the 'we' he referred to might be: Father himself, naturally, and perhaps his elderly housekeeper who lived two cottages from him, or perhaps the church itself, if he was talking spiritually, which as a priest of course he must sometimes be obliged to do.

'We don't want you lapsing now, Glynis,' he said and laughed gently, apparently confirming that his emphasis had been on the kindly side.

'Sure now, you're not in a draught?'

Sometimes, his head at an angle in the car, he reminded her of the Pope.

Why should that thought come back to her now, thought Glynis, why now, those very words as spoken by Father Brennan all those years since? It was the first car she'd ever travelled in, after all. That seemed good enough reason to remember it. Was he still there, she wondered, somewhere along the route this September day, steering the little brown car towards some mission, a new-born, a dying parishioner, someone wanting rid of a confession?

If she closed her eyes, it was one of those September days of then, September being one of the months when Sister Agathe was at her busiest, and most pleased to see Glynis. St Gertrude's had a separate door between the outside world and the convent that let you into its garden, a wooden door made from oak, arched and decorated with brass and locked against the outside with a great key that Sister Agathe turned to allow Glynis in. The garden belonged, it seemed, to Sister Agathe alone. It was this small nun who gave the impression that she allowed the other nuns, her sisters in God, to share its produce with her.

Nothing was ever said, but the fact never had to be spoken: if it wasn't for Sister Agathe, the garden would be barren, providing nothing either decorative or consumable.

Because she'd grown up helping dad in the nursery, Glynis had a way with plants. She had loved Septembers, the planting of crocus and grape hyacinth, the last plucking of luscious fruit.

Sister Agathe always said 'Look at all we've done! Well done, Glynis' at the end of the day when she let her out by the oak-wooden door.

Chapter Seventeen

In a room, whether at home or at Mrs Freebody's, Perry sees Elsie differently to how he sees her on stage during their professional assignations as Grenville and Elsie. Then, of course, they had Ivor Novello or Lionel Monckton or some such to musically sustain the veneer of life-long devotion that audiences expected. Whichever room he's in, whether it's one of their own at home or the one Mrs Freebody has allocated them, there comes a point when Perry can stand no more. It's worse here, though. The bloody wheelchair for a start. At home there is a designated space, or other rooms to park it after Elsie has been removed to another, immovable, location, but anyway Elsie comes with, as it were, her own furniture of the psychological variety, which neither he nor she can escape.

Perry blames her for the way she suggests that being one half of Grenville and Elsie is a minor occurrence, an error of judgement made by Elsie in a rash moment, subsequently regretted. The realisation that this is what she thinks rises bile-like within him. The air is never free of the feeling that what she did professionally prior to meeting Perry (mainly understudying, if truth were known, and she never went on except once at Weston-super-Mare when they cancelled the second half anyway) was superior, and now, once again after so long a gap of time being among other theatricals, her least appealing, almost repugnant, characteristics rise to the surface like long-dormant sludge. Perry knows it's been a personal and professional mistake to come to Cromer, and suspects she knows it too, although there can never be a conversation between them around the doubt.

By the time they returned to the lodgings after the first night, it was almost midnight, Elsie having insisted on staying on to share the hospitality provided for the fire brigade's charity event, but the butter hadn't been easily spreadable on the bread rolls which had curled from being too long in the open air, and the ham had transparent lakes of embedded gristle that got into the cracks of her dentures. Although she'd got Perry to plant her in a conspicuous position to which all eyes might have turned, only one audience member had recognised her, before realising she had mistaken her for Hattie Prince. That, of course, was another bugbear. Our Miss High and Mighty Prince had made it quite clear to Glynis that she did not attend parties of any description, and that she had no intention of attending one at which supporting artistes would be present.

'No, dear, I don't think I'll come, if you don't mind,' Hattie told her. 'I find after my performance I've given what I've given to the best of my ability. I don't want to spoil it by giving a sort of private show afterwards.'

She's a wily one, thought Glynis. The rest of the company wouldn't like it, supposing that Hattie thought herself above the common herd. This was not true. In the Great War, Hattie had undergone exhausting tours of France to entertain the troops, almost to the frontline before word came from the authorities back home that the government would be in deep trouble if the British people knew Hattie Prince had been put in harm's way. In England, she travelled all over to the military hospitals to which the injured and dying soldiers from God knew which of the terrible battles had been sent, sitting by their beds, singing them songs, slapping them on their backs (gently, for they were often feeble), dressed as they once had been in battle-dress and singing 'Piccadilly Lily' (the one they always wanted to hear), and 'Oh Percy, Just Wait Till You Come Home!' about a nervous little imaginary soldier who clearly wasn't much to write home about in the sexual department but finds himself reinvigorated when he gets back to Blighty, mostly in one crucially important piece. Glynis, who had even begun to warm to England's Last Male Impersonator, accepted Hattie's reasoning at face value. She's not as hard as she's painted, Glynis thought, but all trace even of the paint had gone. When Glynis sees Hattie saying her goodnight to the stage door keeper (and Hattie never fails, courtesy to her professional associates, down to the lowliest cleaner, being a perquisite) to intents and purposes, she's Mrs McPhee again, late of 'Evermore'.

'And where's my little soldier?' Hattie calls, turning to see if Gordon is about.

'Reporting for duty,' says Gordon, who's been reading Biggles when Grenville and Elsie were on, and dodges out of the way if he sees so much as a spoke of Elsie's wheelchair. The boy's grown to admire Hattie.

'Time for our route march!' Hattie says, and she and Gordon link arms.

Glynis stands and watches them walking up the pier, at the landing-stage of which Dimple waits at the wheel of the Rolls Royce, ready to whisk one of the once greatest of music-hall's stars back to Darting Hall.

Perry wished he could escape the after-show beano as easily, but he had Elsie to mind, and it had been a difficult evening on stage. With the tabs down, he'd got her chair on at the right angle, but one of the wheels locked en route, so that when the lights went up Perry was kneeling at the side of the chair trying to unwedge Elsie, sitting with her back to the audience. It seemed an unsuitable moment for her to break into 'Only A Rose' when 'He Had To Get Under, Get Out And Get Under' might have been more relevant. Perry released the obstinate brake just in time to serenade her with 'Oh, What A Beautiful Morning', by which time she had managed to twist the top half of her body towards the audience. Imitating the rhythm of the surrey with a fringe on top struck Perry as totally absurd. Audible titters erupted, bouncing from the auditorium on to the stage. Perry wondered if his flies were open, but knew it wouldn't be that. This was the end of the road. This could never happen again. This was what Elsie wanted, and he had been too weak to resist the demand. Was it any wonder that his mind was off and away, running along its old lines?

There are many ways of making love. Which one of them is the best? Tell her the old old story on a dark and stormy night. Tell her the old old story when there is no bright moonlight. You're going to get your girl all nervy when her head's all topsy turvy, then you'll win through properly too if you do, I'm telling you! You'll be in your glory on a dark and stormy night, hold her tight and you will be all right. Let the lightning flash, the thunder roar, she'll hold on to you and she'll holler for more if you tell her the old old story on a dark and stormy night.

Tell her the old old story on a dark and stormy night, Tell her the old old story when there is no bright moonlight. Try the caveman's way of getting a wife, bite her on the neck and she's yours for life, tell her the old old story on a dark and stormy night. Single men? Now then, take the good advice I give to you. Married men? You poor things! Here's a pinch of good advice for you. Hold your YMCA meeting on a dark and stormy night, your Band of Hope and Glory when there is no bright moonlight. You've got to start your sermon early, before your head's all topsy turvy, then a tot or two of whisky will do to pull you through. Phone your wife and tell her it's a dark and stormy night, she's bound to say Oh stay dear, that's all right! Like a henpecked rooster going on strike, you can stay out and do what the devil you like. Tell her the old old story on a dark and stormy night!

So, let's make a night of it tonight, let's make a night of it tonight! I feel as happy as can be, happy as can be, so come along with me. Let's make a night of it tonight, let's see the whole thing through, then home we'll go when the cocks begin to crow, cock cock cock a doodle doo!

Back at Mrs Freebody's, Elsie is strangely quiet. They've brought the flask of coffee Mrs Freebody sent off with them to the theatre, its lukewarm contents the colour of old khaki. Perry pours what is left into the plastic cup, tastes it and passes it to Elsie. She drinks, pulls a face, yawns, says she's all in. For a moment or two, rain tapping gently at the window is the only backdrop.

'I could do with some air,' said Perry.

'Fresh air?' She yawns again, her mouth drawing wider this time, teeth rocking. 'I should have thought you had enough walking back from the theatre. That pier's a route march in itself.'

'It's the lights and the dust and the noise,' Perry explained. 'It gets to me, you know it does. And I'm not getting exercise here, am I? Not real exercise. Not like I get at home.'

'It's late, though.' Elsie looked around for a clock, seeing the hands making their way to eleven o'clock. 'What's the point of going out this time of night? You must want a job! Wait till tomorrow. You can go out for a nice long walk tomorrow.'

'Well, I could, but I feel cooped up. You won't mind if I go out for a stroll, will you? Only to get a breath of air.'

'If that's what you want, of course not, dear. You'd best take a brolly. Doesn't sound as if it's letting up. I've got my *Woman's Realm* to finish.'

He can't get out of the house quick enough, making his way as silently as possible down the curved staircase at the bottom of which Mrs Freebody's dinner gong, its use forbidden for the bed and breakfasters, is silently suspended. At least Perry has a key to let him back in. His insides burn to be free. In a way, what he told Elsie was true, for he cannot be confined, and is intensely relieved to be walking away, almost running, into the street. It would be that this was the moment the heavens opened! He's only been out for a few minutes when the rain intensifies, doesn't stop, and shows no sign of stopping, until, almost as unexpectedly, the downpour is cut off and the air turns soft and fresh, kitten-soft. He furls the umbrella when the rain eases.

The air is always sweeter when he's out and alone. He wandered into a part of the town unexplored since he arrived, well away from the sea, moving so fast that he is short of breath and has to stand in a doorway among a row of unimpressive shops. Above him, gutters dribbled, the pavement glistening black with wet. No, he didn't know this part of the squat town, and by the look of it not many people do, no one much being about.

He finds the perimeter of a park. There's a narrow alley cutting through the parade of shops, a confectioners, a tobacconists, a swinging sign above it flapping lightly against the breeze. Perry fishes in his pockets. His hands are trembling, but steady enough to ease a cigarette from its packet and light it, sucking in the nicotine as if beginning a sacred rite. It is then he sees a man in a trench-coat who's sheltering a little further along in one of the other doorways, a cigarette, ash flicked into the street, in the shadow. The park gates are open. Perry doesn't move, draws up the collar of his coat, but keeps watching. He might walk past the waiting man, stopping for a moment to look into a window of one of the shops, although it is obvious they display nothing of interest. His fingers tingle, the cigarette judders in his fingers. He's about to set off along the row of shops when he sees a man walking out of the park, looking right and left quickly as if needing to adjust himself to the no-moon night.

Oh, what does a sailor care? The storms at sea are rough but gee, there'll be some dirty work tonight. Let it hail or rain or snow, what does a sailor care? If he says I'll kiss the first thing in a skirt I see, well it's awful if the first thing is a Scotsman from Dundee. They're rough, they're tough, they're real hot stuff but their hearts just long for home sweet home, 'cos the time comes when they get fed up with the saucy dames that hang around them with their painted lips and their snaky hips. They pinch your dough and away they go till in the local clink you find them. That's the time they long for their home sweet home and the wife and kids they've left behind them!

Before Perry gets to the man standing in the other doorway the man slips out of the shop doorway, walks across the road and through the park gates. The movement is so quiet that Perry knows the man is fearful of being heard, almost tiptoeing. Now, Perry feels that alteration, the heart in the mouth moment, the time for decision. He could stay waiting in his doorway opposite the park, he could decide to wait until the other man comes out. Of course, he didn't know whether this was the only way in or out of the park. He ought to walk around it to get his bearings, and if only he had time he would, just to make sure, but back at Mrs Freebody's Elsie may have tired of her *Woman's Realm* and be awake when he returns, sitting up in bed and taking notice and wanting details.

He could see no lighting in the park beyond a lamppost outside the gates, and once he'd gone through them he was plunged for a couple of minutes into complete darkness and, more ominously, a midnight silence. He was already as concerned as to how he would get out of the park as to what would happen now that he was in it. The man who'd crossed into the park must be somewhere.

The blood pulses through him, now. If you like to mingle but you want to stay single, just love 'em and leave 'em alone. Don't linger – they'll get you! They're all out to net you, so love 'em and leave 'em alone. Be like the sailor, have one in every port, naughty and haughty but mind you don't get caught, just love 'em and leave 'em alone. At twenty, there's plenty, be careful what you do! At thirty, they're flirty and looking out for you! At forty they're sporty, at fifty they're naughty, at sixty, well, leave 'em alone!

His eyes adjust to the gloom soon enough. Tucked in at the very entrance, hidden from the road behind the greenery that bordered the park, is a dim light above the sign : *GENTLEMEN*. Perry's heart pounds. He had never imagined this, not in Cromer, not when he'd thought this might be a new beginning, a chance to break the habit of a lifetime. It wasn't the same at home. His walks there were different, he needed them, they were the oxygen his life with Elsie couldn't supply.

He had almost to feel his way inside. The light above the entrance didn't reach inside. The sound, regular and rhythmic, of water dribbling from a cistern resounded. He knew this soundtrack. He moved as quietly as he could, but of course he had the noisiest shoes on. He spread the soles of his feet to lessen the impact his moves made, his eyes not yet adjusted to the intense darkness.

As he rounded a corner into what seemed to be the heart of the place, he heard a scuffle. In a park, it might have been a rat or a bird, restless after a day's chirruping, but not here. It was not an alarming rustle; it provided for that moment a new bite of excitement. He waited a little, wanting to know where the sound was coming from. Oh yes, oh yes. The shapes of two men standing side by side merged from out the dark. There was a slight step up to where they stood. The silence was profound, nothing moving in that intense gloom, until one of the men sounded as if he was pulling himself together, and walked, blatantly, without trying to disguise the sound of it, out into the park and, from what Perry could make out, away into the street.

In what was left of this blessed, intimate ceremony, Perry heard the breath of the remaining man, smooth and regular. The moment was elemental. He was conscious of his own breath, wondering what the other man made of it. Tell her the old old story on a dark and stormy night. Tell her the old old story when there is no bright moonlight. Phone your wife and tell her it's a dark and stormy night, she's bound to say Oh stay dear, that's all right! Like a henpecked rooster going on strike, you can stay out and do what the devil you like. Tell her the old old story on a dark and stormy night!

Oh, the thrill! This, Perry knows, is where he belongs for this moment, when the rest of his life falls away like leaves from a tree. He doesn't know what will happen. He almost doesn't care. He knows only that this, at least, is real. He thinks he will wait a few minutes longer, not speaking, not moving, when the other man makes the most sudden of moves, and says 'Good evening, sir.'

CHAPTER EIGHTEEN

It was just gone midnight when Bellairs and Hedgecraft compared notes on the Cromer fatality. Together, they had interviewed the *Forget-Me-Not* company, but it was Hedgecraft who had done most of the donkey work, finding out all they needed to know about the deceased and interviewing Mrs Freebody. The medical officer's report had arrived. Bellairs, stretched by having been put in charge of the investigation into a jewellery theft, turned the pages, its words fusing in his head. He knew Hedgecraft would be ready with a digest of the facts. Sitting across from two cups of coffee brought up from the Norfolk Police HQ canteen, Hedgecraft had almost finished his when Bellairs pushed the report back across the table to him.

'Well, did he or didn't he? Was he or wasn't he? What do you make of it?'

'It's difficult, isn't it? The medical stuff doesn't get us much further. There were no signs of Makepeace having been attacked, no blows inflicted. It's quite clear he didn't drown. He may have been alive when he hit the beach. There was no alcohol in his system. He'd had a light meal a few hours earlier, probably before the show that night. The position of the corpse suggests he fell face down on to the beach. I suppose that means he didn't fall backwards, otherwise he'd have ended facing upwards. Death was almost certainly instantaneous. That's about it.'

'Hmm. Not much to go on. And he still had his wallet on him?'

'Yes. Intact, I think. There was twenty pounds in there.'

'Background?'

'Bit of a blank there, too. Some basics, though. Single, seventy-three years old, one kidney. He was living in Acton, a rented flat over a chippie. I spoke to the landlord. Seems as if he always paid his rent, had been there for several years. Landlord was under the impression he'd done theatre work in London in the past, but he'd been employed as a bingo caller at an amusement arcade for as long as he could remember. I managed to get in touch with the owner. All they could tell me was how he'd asked them for three weeks off to do this job in Cromer. They didn't see why not. He'd quite recently lost his old mother, who he looked after at the flat. He wasn't doing work essential to the running of the British Empire, after all, and they thought he deserved a break. They were expecting him back. But nothing much more there, kept himself to himself, nothing much of friends. One of the company said he'd lost contact with all the people he'd worked alongside in his West End days.'

'What more do we know about his professional life?'

'It's all a bit sketchy, but he seems to have knocked about on the lower rungs of show business for years and then got himself into a big musical at Drury Lane. Chorus work, for Ivor Novello. Ever heard of him?'

'Of course I've heard of him,' said Bellairs, who wasn't going to let on that he didn't care for the man's music or the syrupy lyrics, 'as has every civilised person in the country. He only died a few years ago. Thousands turned out for his funeral. Don't the young know anything?'

'Probably not, sir. Anyway, apparently he carried on appearing in this Novello chap's shows till they came to an end.'

'And went on to further glory as a bingo caller?'

'That's how it goes.'

'How did this Glynis person find him?'

'Contacts. Reputations. I think her boss Monty Desmond, big theatre impresario, knew of him. They had to assemble the show pretty quickly, I understand. And he was probably dirt cheap to hire.'

'They didn't much care for him, the company?,' asked Bellairs. 'That was the impression I got. And remember, he got off to a bad start when the company first met up at the pier. There was this misunderstanding. Makepeace was hired on the understanding that he was a contortionist. Somewhere along the line they had him mixed up with another act of a similar name. He'd walked angrily out of the theatre the day that happened, although he went back, of course. And then, there's the business of him walking out of the show on the night of his death, not staying for his curtain call.'

'Yes, and that surely must be relevant. For a performer to skive off before getting a round of applause – it's completely abnormal in a profession that's all about ego. Anything there, sir?'

'No. There's the evidence of Peregrine Grenville …'

'One of that double act?'

'That's it. So far as we know at the moment, he was probably the last person to see Makepeace alive that night. What we still have no idea about is why Makepeace should have walked out before the end of the show. You're right, Dan. That's the artiste's final moment of glory, isn't it? It's like manna from heaven.'

'Exactly, although I don't think there's much in that. It strikes me not one of them cares a hoot about any of the others. It's such a competitive environment, and this lot have been at it for years. Over time their skins have grown thinner and thinner, along with their blood. No, I didn't get the impression that this was in any way a mutual admiration society. Mrs Freebody …'

'The landlady?'

'A tight little body. Delusions of theatrical grandeur, all that reflected glory. She showed me Makepeace's room. A few cheap toiletries, some underwear, two shirts, a suitcase, and a framed photograph signed "For dearest Heron, Fond Love Always, Ivor". Would that be …?'

'Highly likely,' said Bellairs.

'There is something else, though, sir. Might be interesting.'

'Hmm?'

'A coroner's inquest.' He passed it across the desk.

'Right.'

Bellairs rubbed his eyes, held the document at the appropriate angle for it to focus. 'Belinda Makepeace … Relative of the deceased?'

'His mum. It makes interesting reading.'

'OK. Leave it with me. I've got this damned jewel robbery to sort. I don't suppose you know the difference between opal and sapphire?'

'I should hope I do, sir. I got my fiancée's engagement ring from Woolworths.'

'You get home,' said Bellairs. 'I want to take another look at this Makepeace business before I call it a day.'

'Bit late to call it a day, sir. Past midnight.'

'Best time to get some proper work done in this place. The canteen's closed too, another recommendation. Not much else happening tonight, anyway. Wet weather puts the villains off.'

'There is something, sir. Just came in. Blakiston and Parker brought in a chap they caught in the park. Charge sheet.'

He put the papers on Bellairs' desk, stood in silence, loosening his shirt collar in preparation for the homeward journey. Bellairs put his hand to his face, cupped his chin and sighed, needed a shave. He looked his age, thought Hedgecraft, although he wasn't sure what it was. He hadn't looked at the charge sheet.

'Oh, God. Blakiston's the new chap, isn't he, transferred from Surrey?'

'That's him,' said Hedgecraft.

'He's not wasting time, is he?'

'He's right enough, sir. Doing his duty as only he knows how. Parker was with him.'

'Right.'

Bellairs sighed, stretched his legs beneath the desk, blinked his eyes. He needed more coffee. If Mrs Bellairs had her way they'd never have moved to Norfolk in the first place, and now this.

'I hate these cases,' he said, peering at Blakiston's report with more precision. 'Why couldn't they have dealt with it on the spot? A word in the ear. This,' and Bellairs flipped the paper with his forefinger, 'this makes it official. Had anyone complained?'

'Not that I'm aware of, sir.'

'I mean, if it was broad daylight and kiddies about, that's one thing, but … Why do people behave like that?'

Bellairs set the paper back on the desk and was looking out of the window, across the car park where the modest fleet of police vehicles was neatly lined up ready to be despatched to whatever law-breaking would be available that day.

'Sir. Did you see the chap's name?'

Bellairs pulled himself up in his chair, took up the paper again and refocused his concentration. After a moment, he looked up and across at Hedgecraft, then down at the paper again.

'We had a lot of this in London,' he said. 'Hoped I might have left it behind.'

It was only after Hedgecraft had left the room that Bellairs returned his attention to the coroner's report on Makepeace's mother. It contained plentiful references to Heron Makepeace. From what Bellairs could make out from a quick perusal of the report, this was a woman determined to kill herself, a fate from which, as the coroner's conclusions made clear, her son had saved her. If the coroner had had his way, Heron Makepeace was in line for a medal. She had finally died in her sleep, at home in Acton, and a verdict of natural causes had been recorded. One of her thankfully thwarted attempts at self-annihilation had taken place in Cromer, when her son and a passing life-boatman had saved her from what seemed certain death in a tempest sea.

Bellairs stretched his legs again, felt a muscle go, reached out for the cold dregs of coffee slouched in the cup. The skin floating at its top slid towards him when he lifted it.

There was unfinished business. The desk sergeant told him that Peregrine Grenville was still being interviewed by

Blakiston and Parker. Parker bridled when Bellairs walked into the room without knocking. Blakiston suspected the man he'd nabbed in the park might yet slip from justice.

'I'll have a word with Mr ... Mr Grenville, isn't it?' Bellairs asked, although both of the other officers knew it was not a question, but a statement.

CHAPTER NINETEEN

If I don't write it down (thought Gordon) I shall forget it. Not tomorrow, not for weeks after, but, in time, I shall forget it.

Francis is the writer, the wordsmith (or likes to think he is) but this is what I'm trying to do here, no matter how the words come out: making sure I don't forget. The first thing I must remember is one of the most surprising. Hattie Prince was an extraordinarily handsome woman. I didn't know it then, but I quickly found out. I don't mean beauty queen beautiful. She carried a sense of wholly lovely about her, and it's one of the things about her I can't begin to explain on paper (Francis would be able to). This wasn't what I thought when Francis and I met her that day Glynis took us to Darting Hall. It was a bit like having an audience with royalty, perhaps 'stiff' sums it up, as if we all three of us had to watch our p's and q's, and we'd already almost had an audience with royalty because Lady Darting was there to greet us when we arrived. She seemed very proud that Hattie Prince was staying with her, giving the impression they were old friends, although I know they hadn't clapped eyes on one another until the day before.

Anyway, Hattie had been settled into what looked like a horribly uncomfortable armchair in the Great Hall (I noticed how she kept shifting about as if springs were biting into her) to await our entrance. I have to say that the person we met was a disappointment. It was simply an old woman sitting on a chair with the stuffing (the chair's, obviously) past its best. Nothing special, you'd have thought, not someone you'd stop and look at in the street but, according to everything Glynis and Blodwyn Williams had told us, a great performer. What they call an artiste, with an 'e' that somehow makes it special.

The first thing I noticed was her hat. She was wearing it that day we met her at the Hall, and whenever I see Hattie in my mind's eye, I think I'll always see her in that hat, the one she wore and very seldom took off. When she took it off, we were already three hours into the creation of Hattie Prince the male impersonator. The removal of the hat was one of the very last changes from female to male, that's how it seemed. The taking off of that old-fashioned titfer was a religious procedure, carried out at a particular but never stipulated moment when the magic of her transformation began to crystallise.

Perhaps it's a Victorian or Edwardian thing, women keeping their hats on indoors like that – it was as if she was in church, a sort of Sunday feeling – I don't know (I'll ask Blodwyn, but of course if a man kept his hat on indoors it would be considered a bad do). On top of Hattie's head that hat (always the same one, by the way) might have been a crown. So far as I could tell, it wasn't an expensive hat, nor one she'd picked up at a market stall. A more substantial, comfortable, no-nonsense hat would be difficult to imagine, a sort of twirl of net and felt, like an inverted bowl of fruit with the cherries missing. It's true to say that Hattie would have felt undressed if she hadn't her hat on, and I know for a fact that it was only when she was undressed that she didn't.

Lady Darting introduced Glynis and Francis and me to Hattie, and, beautifully choreographed, Freeman Hardy and Willis (one of the servants at the Hall) brings in a plate of muffins and tea and it wasn't nearly as awkward-feeling as Francis and I had imagined it would be. Now, I noticed Hattie eating. There could be a chapter on this. Over the time I spent with Hattie she didn't actually do much eating in my presence. It was obvious the way she tackled the muffins that it was something she would rather have done in private, and that reminded me of something none of us could deny: she was an old woman. Something about the way she now and again had to chew or move the food about in her mouth made you want to look at her at such moments. The only two things Hattie could do comfortably off-stage were performing and talking about herself, and as the talking was as much a performance as what she did on stage, they were really the same thing.

Anything else, walking, sleeping, and (the muffins had been a hurdle) eating, was best kept from the public gaze, these were functions that were necessary but unperformable. I should say something here anyway about her appearance. Strong jowls, a look of determination about her chin, quite full, fleshy lips, eyes that never seemed to settle long on anything. I should know. I watched her, mostly in the mirror of that dressing room. It made me appreciate I'd done map-reading. It made our relationship quite spooky, mostly communicating with each other's reflection. I learned that it was dangerous to keep looking at yourself in a mirror.

Anyway, going back to Darting Hall and that meeting … Hattie said 'Now, then' and explained why we'd been summoned. She could be very business-like when it suited, although I think she was hopeless about paying bills and probably had stacks of letters demanding payment at home, and I instinctively understood how managers and fellow performers wouldn't want to cross her.

She told us about her sister, Enid. Enid sounded just as extraordinary as Hattie was, although Hattie gave the impression that her sister wasn't half as interesting. Enid had always been her dresser, always with her whenever she was on tour, wherever she worked, all through her career. Enid knew everything that Hattie needed, every move that Hattie made, every ritual that was enacted in her dressing room before every single performance. Enid was there to make sure she had whatever was wanted, always there, combing, brushing, packing, unpacking, finding the number one scarf, passing the tobacco pouch, polishing top hats, buffing the handles of silver-topped canes, laying out the Leichner sticks, setting the hand mirror at the right angle.

'My props, my costumes, the little bits and bobs,' Hattie said, the backbone of her work, her fingers itching at miming the implements and tools of the trade she spoke of. She and Enid had worked as a team all their lives, starting out as a sister act when heaven knows which king was on England's throne, but Enid was unwell and Hattie had insisted she would manage well enough at Cromer without her. This struck me as highly unlikely. I was never convinced that Hattie could cross a road safely without guidance. It also struck me that Enid must have the patience of a saint. She must have been run ragged by Hattie, exhausted by her demands. I'd only been with Hattie, at her side in the dressing room, for a few hours when I pitied anyone charged with looking after this once upon a time star of the halls!

Enid lived in a flat in Pimlico, apparently, and had got Hattie out of a nursing home when Monty Desmond asked if she was available for the Cromer show. It wouldn't have surprised me if she'd got Hattie out of an undertaker's parlour. Someone is on record as saying that only when her coffin was nailed down would Hattie be satisfied. Peace at last! Now, Hattie took the opportunity of making it quite clear there was absolutely nothing wrong with her. She made a go of slapping her chest. I noticed that it slightly winded her, and she'd already almost choked on one of those muffins that day at Lady Darting's.

Glynis stepped in at this point, explaining to Hattie how Francis and I had been drafted in as general dogsbodies (she put it rather more flatteringly than that) and that she felt sure we'd be willing to help as much as we could. Hattie stopped her there and then. No, she said, she didn't want both of us. She wanted one of us, and whichever one of us it was would be helping her, and her alone. One of us was to be her exclusive helpmate. Naturally, I thought Francis would be the lucky (or unlucky, who knows?) one, being older and taller and having that aura of always being the one people wanted if it was a choice between him and me. But she didn't choose Francis. I should have been flattered, but wasn't sure. I felt Francis bristle. 'You're a fine lad,' she said to Francis (I could see he immediately started un-bristling because he always does at the first suspicion of a compliment), 'but you …'

Glynis said 'Gordon' as if to make absolutely sure Hattie knew what she was doing and hadn't chosen the wrong one by mistake. She pointed at me just to make sure.

'Yes, Gordon. Gordon is the one I would like to look after me. You'll have your work cut out, my boy, but you're the smaller and the nippier.'

I didn't think much of this at the time, and Francis said afterwards 'She wants you because you're smaller and nippier. Perhaps she's planning on using you for chimney sweeping.'

At the time, of course, Francis – who frankly isn't over-given to congratulate me on the rare occasions that I show the least sign of being a success – sits there and says nothing, and I sit there not knowing how to feel. Alarmed, probably. Apart from which, I wasn't feeling especially nippy. I knew that 'looking after' Hattie would be some sort of experience, but I would only be needed in the evenings except for matinee days when it would be in the afternoons as well (of course it would, that's what matinee means), and presumably Francis would be just as busy as me for the same periods running about like a scared cat attending to everyone else. I, as Hattie had said, would be exclusive. I didn't necessarily think I'd got the best part of the deal. I consoled myself with the thought that, whatever happened, there would still be plenty of time for Francis and I to enjoy our holiday time, doing the rounds of the churches, brass-rubbing, searching out second-hand bookshops, beach-combing, swimming, and reading. I'm half way through *The 39 Steps* and can't wait to get back to find how Hannay is getting out of another scrape. After all that, looking after Hattie would be a rest cure. Little did I know!

Hattie got straight down to brass tacks.

'I like to be in nice and early.'

I didn't know what she meant.

'*You* won't find your tasks too onerous,' she said, looking at Francis. 'I think you'll find your performers will be at the theatre at the half.'

Did I mishear that? I thought she said 'at the hearth', and for a moment I imagined some sort of theatrical fireplace around which the old artistes gathered to warm their rheumatic joints before going on stage. Later, I found out she'd said 'at the half' which was theatrical parlance for performers arriving at the theatre not less than thirty-five minutes before curtain-up.

'That's not my way,' said Hattie. That determined chin, those cheeks puffed out a little. I began to suspect this might not be an easy ride.

'I like to get to the theatre in good time. I insist on being in my dressing room at least four hours before the beginning of the show.'

She turned her eyes to me.

'We're going to get to know one another,' she said.

Well, I worked this out there and then. That's when I wished she'd have picked Francis. If the evening shows began at 7.30, she wanted me there by 3.30. On matinee days she'd want me there by 11 for a 3 o'clock start. As if this wasn't bad enough, Glynis said after we left that I'd better be at the entrance to the pier every day to escort her to her dressing room when Dimple dropped her off in the Rolls Royce. That would probably add another half hour to my duties. My seaside adventure and the opportunity to explore the beauties of Poppyland were ebbing away before my very eyes. Some holiday this was going to be! I noticed that Francis looked more cheerful after learning of my considerable commitments. John Buchan, Biggles, and not for the first time Ginger, would have to take a back seat in the cockpit of life.

So, as you can see, my experience of *Forget-Me-Not* was quite different from Francis' experience. Basically, on the evening show days I was with Hattie for seven and a half hours, on matinee days for twelve, a length of time spent with one other person to which none of us should ever be exposed. I should say now, before I forget, that for this slave labour (that's how it seemed to me at the beginning and seems still) I received no gift of any kind from Hattie, at least not the sort of gift you buy and wrap up and hand over and hear someone say 'Ooh, how kind' when they see what it is. I don't mind admitting that I now and again wondered if there would be some sort of thank you at the end. A ten bob note would have been nice.

I suppose I didn't realise at the time (and Francis would doubtless put all this much better and knows the sort of words to use and how to arrange them so people get weepy reading them) that the gift she gave me (it wasn't a ten bob note) was much more precious. Of course, she can't have known this, because it wasn't something that could be wrapped up, just something I felt had happened to me because of being with her. I suppose she was what people call self-centred. I was never sure that she cared about anyone else. There's that question mark over Enid, really. Poor old Enid had done what I was trying to do for two weeks for most of a century. I couldn't imagine what all that devotion, always never putting herself first, must have done to her.

In fact, one of the big regrets I had about the whole thing is that I had never met Enid. She'd been on the halls too, in her early days, singing and foot-juggling although not, I think and quite sensibly, at the same time. Hattie had old photographs she carried around with her. Enid had been a pretty girl, but had given up the profession when Hattie became a star, and devoted the rest of her life to her famous sister, sharing what rags and tatters of it that were left over with a husband of her own (hers lasted, while Hattie's didn't) in Pimlico. There were photographs of the older Enid, too, and you got the impression of a comfortable, easy person. In the more recent photos she looked like a plump may-fly. You got the impression of her fluttering forever around her much more prominent sister. She also looked astonishingly like Hattie. Dress Enid up in Hattie's costumes and you wouldn't have told one from another.

I don't mean that Hattie was selfish. It wasn't that. Francis said the rest of the performers thought she was stuck-up, but I don't think Hattie had a disregard for them, it was just that she needed all her concentration on what she was about, and she had no shred of doubt about the magic she brought with her onto the stage. If she didn't believe in herself, and invest all that faith in herself, who else would have? So long as she imagined the other performers thought of her differently from how they thought of one another, I think Hattie was happy. But she didn't rehearse alongside the others; Glynis had to see to it separately. I thought this was telling. It was as if whatever she achieved on stage at night in front of the audience had happened with complete naturalness, with no sense of effort or risk of failure. If I ever see such style, such assurance, such elegance again, I'll be lucky. Funny thing is, I think I shall always think of her whenever I look into a mirror, seeing her there, looking back at me, forever as if we both existed somewhere else, apart and beyond ourselves.

I told Francis about one incident. It was one of those afternoons when I was in and out of Hattie's dressing room. I'd told her I wouldn't be back for a bit because Mr Grenville was having trouble with Miss Balls' wheelchair. It had a mind of its own, and he couldn't steer it on stage. It was Francis who was really responsible for looking after everyone else in the cast except Hattie, but he must be one of the least practical people on the planet, so I said I'd take a look at it. It was the least

I could do for Mr Grenville. I felt sorry for him, for several reasons. It was a tricky job, and I almost wrenched my wrist trying to sort it out.

Anyway, when I got back to Hattie, she was reading. She was a little deaf (on purpose, sometimes, I thought) and I don't think she heard me come in. She was reading aloud, but softly, as if to herself. All I caught was something about wimples and crisping pins, and I heard the words 'there shall be stink'. Her voice shook slightly as she murmured the words, but they meant nothing to me. She saw me in the mirror then, and closed the book. It was a bible. She put a towel over it as if she didn't want me to see. It was a bit odd, I suppose, a bit out of character, I thought. Anyway, I mentioned it to Francis, and he pulled a face, did that thing he does that makes you think he's storing something up for later.

Then, of course, I could never forget (and this bit I didn't really have to write down, because I shall always remember it) the most extraordinary ritual of all.

It was the first night of *Forget-Me-Not*. The thing I was most looking forward to was the half hour or so when Hattie would be on stage doing her act. I would be free at last. Some chance!

'Now, love, there's one very special thing,' she said. 'My handbag.'

Up it came from under the table where she always rested it as soon as we arrived in the dressing room. It was a large bag, very solid, age unknown but built, like Hattie, to last.

'My handbag,' said Hattie, as if confirming its existence. I nodded, waiting for more.

'While I'm on stage, I want you to look after it.'

'I won't leave the room,' I said.

'Oh, no. I want you to stand in the wings, dear, in the prompt corner, where I can see you. Whenever I look offstage, I need to see you there, holding my handbag.'

She seemed to brush this off, as if it really wasn't important at all, but I knew better. Of all the things I had to do, this was the one thing of all, the crowning of the ritual. So it was that whenever Hattie was on stage, I followed her into the wings and waited there, her handbag held up as if I was auctioning a Rembrandt at Christies.

For two weeks, my arms ached.

CHAPTER TWENTY

'You're a good runner, Mr Grenville' said Blakiston. 'I'll give you that. Chasing off like a teenager.'

Blakiston and Parker had manhandled Perry into the police van after pulling him down in a running tackle as he'd taken off through the park. There had been no reasonable possibility of escape. He'd tripped in the dark over some edging along the paths, Blakiston and the other man on top of him, putting his arm behind his back, pushing his face into the meaty earth. All Perry could hear was the man's voice echoing in the public lavatory.

'Good evening, sir. I'm arresting you for importuning for immoral purposes in a public place.'

They were words he'd waited almost a lifetime to hear.

Not much more was said en route to the police station. If it was said, Perry didn't hear. The station must have been close by. A polite policeman at the desk took details of Perry's name, his address. Perry emptied his pockets, signed a form. He was shown into a room where a table separated three chairs. He was shaking, uncontrollably, his mind juddering. What way out was there out of what must follow? Blakiston looked to be in his twenties, quite sharply dressed, plain-clothes but not so plain, his hair brylcreemed slick, artfully wayward strands left dangling over his forehead. Parker, the one Perry thought had pushed his face into the ground, was middle-aged, verging on burly.

'Just to remind you, sir,' said Blakiston, 'that we have arrested you this evening for importuning for an immoral purpose. You entered the public lavatory in the park at 10.55, and were apprehended ten minutes later. You were loitering at the stalls for a total of eight and a half minutes. Can you explain your presence in the park lavatory at that time of night?'

What could he say? Age might yet be on his side.

'Good lord! Why do you think people usually go to the lavatory?'

'That's what I'm waiting to learn, sir.'

'It was a cold night. I needed to pass water.'

'There must have been a lot to pass. Nearly nine minutes worth. Sergeant Parker' (Blakiston vaguely looked in the direction of the older man) 'observed you looking around and once moving away from the stalls and then returning to them.'

Parker leant his elbows on the table, moving his head close to Perry's. For a moment, Perry thought the man might lash out at him, but the man was smiling, crooked as it was.

'Married man, are you, Mr Grenville?'

'Yes.' He waited a second. 'Actually, not officially married, exactly, no, but Miss Balls … Elsie, my partner.'

'You're a visitor here, I see,' said Blakiston, looking down at the papers.

'Yes.'

'An actor, yes?'

'Well, not an actor. Not really. A singer, I suppose you'd say. A performer. I'm working on the pier at present. Do

180

you really think I would be stupid enough to do what you're suggesting?'

'Oh, nothing surprises us, sir. We've heard everything. The location at which you were detained is well known as a place where certain behaviour occurs.'

'Certain behaviour? Is that police-speak?'

'I don't think you want to try clever cuts with us, sir. It's an unsavoury business. We take no pleasure in it.'

'I want to speak to a solicitor.'

Perry had heard this demanded in dramas that had played along such lines, but had no idea of how he might afford one.

'That can be arranged, sir,' said Parker, as if this would make very little difference. 'Your partner ... Elsie, is it? She's in for a bit of a shock, isn't she?'

'It would kill her,' said Perry. 'She's far from well. In a wheelchair. She depends on me.'

'Well, we should think of these things before we do something stupid, shouldn't we?'

'The thing is,' said Blakiston, 'if you'd have walked out of that place a couple of minutes before, I wouldn't have arrested you.'

'So why have you? You have no evidence.'

'You ever been had up for this sort of malarkey before?' asked Parker.

'Of course not.'

'We're checking you out. If there've been any convictions or cautions we'll find them.'

'You'll be able to explain it all to the magistrates, but they're not born yesterday, sir. Perhaps you'd better telephone Elsie. She'll be waiting up for you, like as not. You are entitled to make a telephone call.'

'And there's the show. I'm on stage for the rest of the week.'

'Once we're done with the formalities, you'll be free to go. The case will come up in a few weeks.'

'Just as well,' said Parker. 'You wouldn't want it getting into the papers when you were appearing on stage every night, would you? Tad awkward.'

'In some cases,' said Blakiston, 'we have to ask you to undertake a physical inspection. An unpleasant procedure for all concerned. Based on the events witnessed earlier this evening, I don't think we need put you through that particular indignity.'

'You're lucky,' said Parker, although his expression didn't suggest celebration. 'If you had given us reason to instigate a medical you would have been in even more trouble.'

CHAPTER TWENTY ONE

The first view that Hattie Prince had of her unexpected visitor was the woman's reflection in the dressing room mirror, a reflection that somehow deflected whoever came into Hattie's presence. Gordon wondered what percentage of Hattie's life had been spent looking into those mirrors, keeping her safe, at a distance, seeing life in reverse. But this, he could tell at once, was different, as if Hattie was looking through the mirror rather than at it. Whether she recognised what she saw he could not know, but after what seemed long moments she turned her face into the room.

'Yes,' said the woman. 'It's quite extraordinary. It hardly seems possible, but … I think we've met before.'

Gordon gently closed the dressing room door behind her, subduing the offstage hubbub. He stood smilingly between the two women, as if they were generals arrived at the signing of a truce.

'Forgive me,' said Hattie, with no shred of forgiveness in her voice. The portcullis she could put up without warning had been raised. 'I don't recall.'

'This is Mrs Taylor,' said Gordon.

'You have the advantage of me,' said Hattie.

'Mrs Taylor and I spoke briefly during the interval. She asked if it might be possible to see you, and I said you'd be delighted.'

'Ah.' Hattie didn't sound too sure. 'Mrs Taylor. I hope you enjoyed the show?' Well, she might as well make the best of a bad job.

There being no other choice, Gordon drew up a bentwood chair and invited the guest to sit. He placed it close by the dressing table rather than across the room, as if Hattie and her visitor were old friends longing for a renewed closeness.

'I mustn't stay long. My daughter-in-law brought me. It's our birthday tomorrow – we share the same date – so we've treated one another. We're on holiday at West Runton.'

Hattie, unacquainted with geography or the niceties of family life, gave a smile that suggested she understood, not that she'd ever been on anything resembling a holiday.

'It was so unexpected. After almost fifty years, out of the blue. As soon as you came on at the beginning, I knew. I had my doubts, obviously. I thought, no, it can't be. Things like that don't happen. But they do.'

'Things like what don't happen?' asked Hattie.

'All through the first half I was wondering, couldn't concentrate on anything but asking myself if I was right. And, of course, when you came on at the end, then I knew, but I'd made up my mind by then.'

'I think,' said Gordon, 'Mrs Taylor realised that you and she had met before.'

There was a pause before Hattie reluctantly interrupted.

'And where was that?'

'Oh, I can tell you exactly. At the Camberwell Empire in 1910.'

Gordon was watching Hattie's face. As if stamped in place, her expression had not altered, although she was looking directly into the woman's eyes.

'Mrs ... Taylor, did you say?'

'Of course, I wasn't married then. I was Ethel Braund. And please, do call me Ethel. We met for the merest moment. In fact, I don't think I told you my name.'

'Perhaps you could tell us your story, Mrs Taylor ... Ethel ... how you came to meet Miss Prince? Fifty years ago?'

'Yes, half a century ago. It was the end of January, or the beginning of February – I don't remember exactly. 1910. I was working as a milliner in London, at one of the smaller department stores off Oxford Street. It was a very cold night. I'd arranged to meet my aunt for supper at Lyons Corner House in the Strand. She'd put the wrong day in her diary. I waited outside. Eventually, I wondered if she'd arrived earlier and already gone into the restaurant, but when I went in I couldn't see her or a table that I might have to myself. I was on the point of leaving when a nippy said a woman had invited me to join her if I wouldn't mind sharing.'

'I don't understand. Was that woman me?' asked Hattie.

'Oh, no. Quite unlike you, really, and yet, in her way, very like.'

'How confusing,' said Hattie.

'She introduced herself as Connie. "Oh, Connie's been around, dear!" she said. I didn't quite know what she meant by that, although I had a suspicion. She told me she was on the halls, the music-halls, singing.'

Gordon was watching Hattie. She raised an eyebrow that suggested she had never heard the name. Ethel looked to Gordon as if seeking permission to continue.

'I'd never met anyone like her. She was someone quite outside the range of my experience. I hardly recognise the person I was then.'

'Strange,' said Hattie. 'Odd, when you say you recognised me. Not that I've come into your story yet.'

'Oh no, you weren't there, not at Lyons Corner House. This woman – Connie – I can't remember her mentioning any surname, and I'm sure she wouldn't have remembered my name, she was the sort of person who'd forget something like that almost at once because it was obvious she wasn't interested in other people, and anyway I've never been the sort of person that people are interested in. But this woman … She overflowed with life, brash, noisy, dazzlingly colourful, like a bird of paradise that had flown off-course and landed in a tea-room. Her fingers were fat, with rings. My life and hers were so obviously different. I'd been very strictly brought up. It's almost embarrassing to think how narrow-minded I was, almost no experience of the world, and suddenly to be bombarded with information about the sins of the universe by this woman who seemed to have sucked everything out of life that she could get … how would I forget that?'

'How indeed,' said Hattie, but with a sense of not wanting to give anything about herself or her own life away.

'She overcame me, I suppose, her vibrancy, so much to say about her work and her career on the music-halls and her husband – he was called Peter, I remember, and was a dentist, I think, or some sort of quack doctor, so far as I could make out. So much detail, far more than I needed to know and much more than I could understand. I sat through as much of it as I could, but I knew I had to get away from her. She was the most blatant example of temptation I had ever faced, someone who reeked of all I'd been warned of, but had never been allowed even a glimpse of, and here she was, this rowdy extravagant creature opening the doors of immorality. The heat of the room, the noise, the smell of her cigarettes, the fog of her cheap perfume. I had to get away from it. And that's when it happened.'

'When *what* happened?' asked Hattie, but Gordon could see she knew.

'I took the wrong bag.'

CHAPTER TWENTY TWO

Expressionless, Hattie looked back at her.

'The wrong bag?'

'Yes,' replied Ethel. 'I'd put it under the table as I sat down. Connie's bag must have been there, too, and when I left I took her bag instead of my own. It was careless of me, very stupid. I'd put my purse in my coat pocket, so I knew I had enough change to pay for my tea, and auntie's if she wasn't feeling generous, and the fare for the tube was in another pocket so it wouldn't get confused with the coins in the other pocket. It was all quite my fault. It hadn't occurred to me that the other woman might have put *her* bag under the table, although now I think of it, I seem to remember seeing her take her bag off the spare chair at her table and putting it by her feet. It wasn't until I got home that I opened the bag, and realised it wasn't my bag at all. The Revd Purchase was nowhere to be seen.'

'Would you have expected to find a parson in your handbag?' asked Hattie.

'Yes. The Revd Purchase's two volume publication, *Climbing to Righteousness*, took up much of the space. His books were my constant study.'

'How inconvenient for you,' said Hattie, 'and for the other woman …'

'Yes. Poor Connie. The strange thing was, her bag was so like mine, the feel of its handle, the shape of it, and exactly the same shade of grey, that you might understand how such a mistake occurred, and because I didn't examine it closely or attempt to open it until I was ready for bed, I was at a loss as to what I could do to immediately rectify the error.'

'It must have been a nasty shock,' said Gordon. 'Ladies' handbags are precious and highly personal accessories.'

'Oh, much more than that,' said Ethel. 'They are the portable support of our everyday lives. Being of a capacious fashion, I had only recently emptied my bag and reorganised its contents. So far as I recall, at the time of the misunderstanding, it contained no personal information, no details of my name or address or so forth. I could only imagine the panic the poor woman would have felt on finding her handbag had been taken – stolen by me, for all she might think! By then, of course, it was really too late to return it that evening. I made a cup of cocoa to calm myself, and worked out a plan. I had no address for Connie, but during her exhaustive account of her doings she made sure to tell me she was appearing at the Camberwell Empire. Third turn, she said, I distinctly remember that because I had no idea what she meant. Third turn … It was the only information I had. After work the next day, I took a bus to Camberwell and found the theatre.' She looked up at Hattie, her eyes narrowing. 'And that I think is where we met.'

'Really?' asked Hattie.

'On arrival at the Empire, I enquired of the stage doorkeeper if I might see Connie. He stared at me blankly. There was no one there of that name, he said. By this time I was quite agitated, thinking of the loss not only of my bag but of the other woman's bag being in my possession. Come what may, I must somehow get my bag back and restore the one I had deprived her of. Of course, I couldn't understand why the stage door-keeper didn't know who I was talking about. I described the woman I had met, and at last saw a flicker of recognition. Yes, he said, I know who you mean, but he didn't know where the Connie came into it. I explained there had been a muddle with our handbags and it was a matter of urgency that I should return Connie's – and retrieve my own which she must surely have taken from the tearoom. He laughed and said "If you find her, let me know. The manager wants a word with her." He pointed me to a door that led into a corridor and a flight of stone steps up to the next floor, where he said she should have been. Dressing room 6, I think it was. The place was fit for Eskimos. It's a wonder they didn't catch their deaths of cold.

'I knocked at the door of number 6, but there was no answer. I knocked again, and asked if anyone was there. The door of the next room opened. A charming young man, impeccably dressed. A man about town. He asked if he could help. I did my best to explain. He was sympathetic and charming, but, he told me, there was a problem. Connie (he laughed when I mentioned her name, and said 'Oh, she called herself Connie, did she?') was indeed on the bill but, and I remember his words, it had been "a week not without difficulty". And tonight, he said, she hasn't showed up at all, and the management was not amused. He said she'd had her chips.

'This was hardly satisfactory from my point of view. She still had my handbag, and I had hers, and I was no nearer solving the problem. My head was spinning with it all. The young man was most helpful. What if I left Connie's bag with him? She was bound to return to the theatre, probably the very next evening, or even in time for second house later that evening, and he would make sure her bag was returned to her, and take my details so that she could arrange for my bag to be returned to me.'

'So, tell me, Mrs Taylor,' said Gordon. 'When you realised the bag was not your own, did you examine its contents?'

'Of course. My hope was that it would contain information as to the name and address of its owner, beyond the few facts I had gleaned from our conversation, but her handbag, like mine, contained no personal details as to who she might be.'

'What did it contain?'

'Well ... The only *information* it contained was a text.'

'Text?'

'A biblical quotation. It struck me so forcibly. I have never forgotten it, perhaps word for word. It ended "It shall come to pass ..."'

'It shall come to pass...'

Their heads turned to where Francis was standing at the open dressing room door. His words, words that Francis sounded so biblically, cut through the space.

'"It shall come to pass,' he said, 'that instead of a sweet smell there shall be stink". It's from Isaiah, Chapter Three. I believe Dr Crippen put that text into his wife's handbag as a warning to her. Throughout his childhood in Coldwater, Michigan, Dr Crippen's head had been filled with the Old Testamaent. Isaiah was his favourite prophet. He never forgot. It's highly likely that Isaiah's words left him with a lifelong fascination for women, frightful as those words are. And when Gordon told me he'd overheard Miss Prince reading from Isaiah – I recognised some of the words – I immediately thought of Dr Crippen, and how Miss Prince had known his wife.'

Nobody moved. The silence went on for several moments, until the woman who had begun the quotation spoke.

'Yes. It shall come to pass. Those are the very words. They affected me horribly. I felt tainted, as if … as if evil had somehow reached out and touched me. I had to rid myself of that bag. I snapped it shut and never opened it again. But … how could you know?'

'My apologies,' said Francis, 'but Gordon really must take more care in shutting doors effectively. I happened to be passing as he was trying to do so, and didn't move on.'

'Listening at doors now?' suggested Gordon, making a vague tut-tutting noise. 'Mrs Taylor, this is my cousin Francis.'

'Delighted to meet you, Mrs Taylor. Forgive me for interrupting, Miss Prince. Gary told me to wait in the corridor while he went back to his room to fetch some things. Your conversation was so interesting that I couldn't tear myself away.'

'He doesn't always give such a bad impression of himself,' said Gordon. 'And the noble art of eavesdropping probably goes back to the beginning of Time itself.'

Despite the invasion of her dressing room, that hallowed space to which only Gordon had been freely admitted and that he had come to appreciate as a rare, untroubled sanctuary where ritual and perfection met, Hattie was as relaxed as he had ever seen her. It was unusual enough for her to subside into silence, and now a sort of restfulness, contentment almost, glowed around her, as if she were approaching the end of a weary journey.

'To give Gordon credit,' said Francis, 'I don't think *he* would sink so low as to listen at doors, but it may yet be to everyone's advantage that my reputation for impeccable conduct has temporarily gone West. I wonder if I might be allowed to help.'

'Another chair,' said Hattie.

Chapter Twenty Three

Francis knew how to sit when observed by others. If nothing else, it was something he'd learned from standing in the wings of *Forget-Me-Not*, seeing how Hattie Prince stood, sat, removed a hat, adjusted a scarf, cast her head. Throughout the run, he had also watched Gordon standing beside him in the prompt corner when Hattie was on stage, holding Hattie's handbag high as if he were a taxi-driver waiting for a client at an airport arrival lounge. He'd seen how Gordon shifted position depending on where Hattie moved, always making sure she could see the bag whenever she looked for it.

'Miss Prince, for whom I have the very greatest respect and admiration, almost certainly made the right decision in choosing Gordon over me as her helpmate and confidante. Smaller and nippier, I believe, were the reasons given.'

'And less liable to snoop outside half-closed doors,' added Gordon.

'Point taken. Vulgar and over-used as the expression is, I can confirm that Gordon is what is known as salt of the earth.'

'Gordon's a grand boy,' said Hattie. 'He's been wonderful. Couldn't have managed without him. And talk! Oh, how we've talked, eh, love?'

'Due to his, shall we say, considerable commitment to Miss Prince, Gordon hasn't had much spare time, Mrs Taylor. He hasn't got through a single mind-bending chapter of Captain W E Johns all week, so it isn't all bad news. Normally, or perhaps abnormally, he is agonising about some crisis concerning Ginger's predicament in the cockpit. We can only hope that his duties on Cromer Pier have broken the habit. I, on the other hand, have been less in demand, making cups of tea and ironing the odd costume – some of them distinctly odd – and helping the rest of the company however I could. I admit I was a little put out not to have been selected for' (and he glanced at Hattie) 'special duties, but in retrospect, I think Miss Prince made the right choice.

'As it happens, things turned out for the best. It gave me time to do some research into the history of music-hall. I had never imagined I'd be interested, indeed I knew nothing about it, but I'd heard a radio programme that lit the spark. I wanted to immerse myself in it. What a forgotten world! But it was you, Miss Prince, who convinced me it would remain a passion for the rest of my life. When I saw you striding down the pier, coming on stage and embracing the audience as one, when I saw your brilliant technique and extraordinary style and the way you lived a different life when your number came up, I knew I was watching the essence of music-hall.

'It was after the first night that I asked our Branlingham librarian's help in reading up on the subject. Uncle Billy brought a couple of books to the Old Fishergirl's Cottage. My head for the past week has been full of Wilkie Bard, Marie Lloyd, Gertie Gitana, Harry Champion, George Leybourne. So many wonderful performers and characters. One of the most infamous and tragic was what used to be known as a serio-comedienne. Her stage name was Belle Elmore.'

Ethel looked to Hattie for enlightenment. Where was this going? The boy who listened at doors barely made sense.

'Your description of the woman you met at Lyons Corner House, her forthright characteristics, her gaudy appearance, the American twang in her speech, the talk of her career and of her marriage to a man called Peter … and this happening at the end of January 1910 … Bear those facts in mind. Over the teacups she chattered on and on, but never gave you her full name, although introducing herself as Connie. She did however mention that she was third turn at the Camberwell Empire. I think it was the last day of January, 1910. I looked up the list of performers who played that week at the Camberwell Empire and – sure enough – among the artistes was Mrs Crippen, appearing as Belle Elmore. I also realised that this had been the last week of that unfortunate woman's life. And there was something else, too … According to the records I have seen, another, far superior, performer, was booked for the Camberwell Empire that week.'

Francis was looking into space. He had left the gap into which only one of those in the room could step.

'Well, I had a free week,' said Hattie. 'In the normal run of things I wouldn't have been seen dead at the Camberwell Empire. You didn't get ovations there, you got pneumonia and probably fleas, but I'd nothing else booked. The very next week I was on the bill at the Holborn Empire. I was slumming at Camberwell.'

'Then it *was* you I met', said Ethel. 'The young man, the handsome, immaculately dressed young man-about-town who took charge of that handbag? It was you!'

'Yes,' said Hattie. 'It was me. I wanted to explain, but you were in such a state. You fled.'

'It was the text. Those dreadful words. They chilled me, as if I'd been defiled. But it wasn't just the words, you see. There was … something else.'

'Yes,' said Francis. 'I thought there must be.'

'Oh, it was terrible. Of course, as soon as I realised I'd taken the wrong bag I had to open it, of course I did, and there was the text and then, deep inside the bag … it glowed, it shone, it dazzled. The brilliance of the light almost blinded me. It was as if I was staring at the sun, staring at it although you know you shouldn't, that it will do you harm, that you should look away before it's too late and you're blinded for ever.'

'Jewels?' asked Francis.

'Jewels. Jewels beyond anything I could ever had imagined. I felt tainted, a thief, as much a thief as if I'd put a brick through a jeweller's window and made off with the swag. I had never seen such splendour, rings and brooches and necklaces. The brightness of those diamonds! I shook with fear. Something deep within me wanted to explore this treasure that had mistakenly fallen into my hands, to run my fingers through it, to fasten the brooches to my blouse, to drape myself in the pearl and diamond necklaces, the emeralds, the sapphires, but I knew that that way was the path to Hell. The only thing I wanted in the world that night was to rid myself of that dreadful handbag, and those horrible words that threatened me with an unspeakable fate. Those evil, terrifying words.'

They sat, still, feeling the coolness of the room grow chillier, as if the icy cold of the decrepit Camberwell Empire had blown in for a moment to add a genuine whiff of the long-gone past.

'Gordon, dear,' said Hattie. 'Fetch the bag.'

CHAPTER TWENTY FOUR

There wasn't much fetching to be done. The handbag was stored in a little cupboard beneath Hattie's dressing-table. With the dull tread suitable for what he knew was a significant moment, Gordon removed it and handed it to Hattie. Ethel gasped, putting a handkerchief to her mouth as if to close up the shock.

'My bag!' she cried. 'It's my bag!'

'I'm afraid not,' said Hattie. 'You see. It only goes to prove how alike the two bags must have been, and how easy it was to muddle them. This is the bag you took by mistake when you left Lyons Corner House. This was Belle Elmore's bag.'

She turned to Gordon.

'You can open it now, love. It's time it was opened. Let the air in. Open it and read it.'

The gentle click of the clasp was surprisingly quiet for a clasp that hadn't been undone for half a century. Gordon reached into it, removed a printed card, and read.

'"The Lord will smite with a scab the crown of the head of the daughters of Zion, and the Lord will discover their secret parts."'

He looked up, as if wondering whether to continue.

'Go on, love,' said Hattie.

"'In that day the Lord will take away the bravery of their tinkling ornaments about their feet … the bonnets, and the ornaments of the legs, and the headbands, and the tablets, and the earrings, the rings, and nose jewels … the mantles, and the wimples, and the crisping pins, the glasses, and the fine linen, and the hoods and the veils, and it shall come to pass, that instead of a sweet smell there shall be stink.'"

For a while it was as if an impenetrable veil had been drawn over them, suffocating and frightful.

'It sends a shiver down your spine,' said Hattie. 'It's Isaiah. Chapter Three.'

She reached out her hand to the other woman, resting it on her arm gently.

'I owe you an explanation, Ethel. All those years ago, I should have introduced myself properly. I should have explained who I was. I should have said, 'Call me Hattie'. Let me say it now, half a century later. Call me Hattie. The fact is, I have no idea what happened to your bag. I left it in Cora's dressing room, for her to collect when she returned to the theatre. I always knew her as Cora. Connie, as she called herself when you met. It was one of the many names she liked to be known by. Her real name was Kunigunde Mackamotzki. Polish. Of course, that would never have looked good in lights and think of the bulbs you would need, so she'd translated it into Connie. She had a name for every occasion. On stage, of course, she was Belle Elmore. Poor Belle. The night you came to Camberwell, she hadn't turned up for the shows. We thought she'd been on the booze and was laid up somewhere. She didn't return to the theatre. I took her bag, the one you gave me, back home at the end of the week, as I was expecting to meet her a few days later at

199

a Ladies Guild meeting, but from what I remember no–one ever saw her again. Her husband Dr Crippen said she'd gone abroad suddenly, and at first there seemed no reason to doubt him. He didn't appear in the least interested in my returning her handbag to him, so I decided to keep it until I met her again. And then the weeks went by with not a sign or a word from her, and I didn't think of the bag. It was summer before they found her body in the cellar at Hilldrop Crescent.'

Francis leaned forward and smiled at Mrs Taylor.

'I think the day you had your unexpected tea party at Lyons Corner House with Belle Elmore, alias Kunigunde Mackamotzki, alias Cora Turner, alias Mrs Crippen, alias Connie, was her last. She never returned to the theatre to collect her bag. Yours, Mrs Taylor, fell victim to the chaos of theatrical life with its constant coming and goings, and with no means of knowing to whom it belonged, it was always unlikely that you would ever be reunited with it. And, all unknowingly, you played your supporting role in one of the most notorious cases in criminal history.'

'It's beyond belief,' said Ethel. 'That she was murdered by Dr Crippen … that I met her that evening, just before … just before …'

'Just before the end, yes.'

'But the bag … and the jewels? I don't understand.'

'When you left me with Belle's handbag that night,' said Hattie, 'I went back to my dressing room and opened it. How extraordinary that I should have had exactly the same reaction as you. The words and the jewels. They stared back at me accusingly, as if I'd sinned against the world and there, too, were the clusters of diamonds, the sapphires, the emeralds, the turquoise, the ropes and ropes of pearls.'

'Oh, there can be little doubt. If I may.' Francis took the bag, almost caressed it, and peered deep within it as if it were an Aladdin's cave.

'No doubt at all,' he said after a moment. 'These are the property of Belle Elmore.'

'They can't be,' said Ethel. 'It's amazing. But how do you know?'

'It came out at the Old Bailey trial when Crippen was tried for her murder. Here, you see.' The jewels ran through Francis' fingers. 'This is the notorious "Rising Sun" brooch, bursting with brilliant rays of light, that Belle loved to wear as a corsage. And these garters, peppered with diamonds. Look at these, opal I think, and sapphire. There are studio portraits of Belle adorned with these very items. They meant more to her than could children of her own. And they were her insurance against her husband and against her professional failure.'

'But why?' asked Ethel. 'That's what I don't understand, Hattie. Why, after all these years, have you kept them?'

'What else would you suggest?' asked Hattie. 'I didn't know what to do with them. It was months before I knew Crippen had murdered Belle. I didn't know her well, but we rubbed along together whenever we met. It would be kind of me to tell you what a brilliant artiste she was, but she wasn't. It wasn't that she was hopeless on stage. There was some talent there, but so small, nothing came across. People put up with her, that's all you could say. I never had cause to complain about her. By the time the news came out about how Crippen had done her in, I'd rather forgotten about her handbag. And the words of that text you know, that ghastly voice as if God was speaking to you directly from among that horde of gold. And what good would it have done to hand the jewels in and get mixed up with the police and have to stand as witness? No. I'd left it all too late. I wanted none of it. If I gave the jewels away, they might be traced back to me, or if I sold them. And then, as the years went by, they became my insurance. It shames me to admit it, but it's true. You'll be all right, old girl, I told myself. They can pass you by, they can go crazy for their pop singers and their rock and roll, they can change their taste as many times as they want, they can give you the bird and the cold shoulder and managements can give you the old heave-ho, but you've got all this … all this wonder. I'm not proud of it. I don't expect you to understand. Five cows' lengths from a slaughterhouse, that's where I came from, that's what I fought my way out of, and there was no way I was ever going back.

'Ethel,' said Hattie, and she was still clasping the woman's hand in her own, something Francis had never imagined Hattie ever doing to another. 'In a way, you know, the handbag and all it holds is as much yours as mine. Finders keepers, after all. Why don't you take it? Take it. In lieu of your lost handbag.'

'How kind of you, Hattie, really it is. I'm a little tempted, I suppose, but no, I don't think so. It's all so long ago, and really, I have everything I want in life. Besides which, I see now that it has nothing to do with me, and that wretched handbag has hung about you all these long years, an albatross. I think you have suffered more. I would not have wanted it by me day and night.'

'I think you may be right. I have been frightened of it, terrified that I would lose it, that it would be taken from me, on tenterhooks in case I might carelessly stow it somewhere out of sight under a table and someone else, thinking it to be their handbag, took it away by mistake. One way and another, it has been a curse to us both, and I may have got the worst of it.'

'This may be the moment to make my second confession,' said Francis. 'The sort of people who listen at doors may at least once in their lives be unable to resist looking into a lady's handbag when she isn't around.'

Gordon's face darkened, his voice thundered.

'Francis! You didn't? You haven't?'

'I don't know how I would have felt if my inquisitiveness had been in vain. Believe me, I considered the matter carefully. As it happened, things fell into my hands.'

'I think you'd better explain,' said Gordon.

'It was the fact that I've been the general dogsbody around here for the last two weeks. If ever I'm sold as a slave in a Persian market I shall at least have some idea of what sort of future lies ahead. Anyway, I probably hit rock bottom last week when the theatre cleaner went off sick and I had to do the dressing rooms. It was the morning after the first night fire brigade charity event. Miss Prince was invited to an after-show celebration in the bar.'

'Oh, I hate those things,' said Hattie. 'I never go to them.'

'Pardon me for suggesting it, but isn't it more a case of your keeping up the idea that you never make such off-stage appearances, rather than not making them? You were certainly in the bar that night. The firemen were all over you.'

'In a manner of speaking,' added Gordon.

'You must have changed quickly after the show. You were in the bar five minutes after the curtain came down.'

'Yes. Perhaps on that occasion I gave in. I shouldn't have. I went back to the dressing room to get my things after I'd spent a bit of time chatting with the boys, but it was locked. There was no one to unlock it.'

Francis nodded.

'When I arrived the next morning in my temporary capacity as the theatre cleaner, I got the keys from the doorkeeper and set to work. As soon as I opened the door of your room I could see you'd left the place in a hurry.'

'Yes. They were pestering me to join them in the bar. I'd never have left the room in that state. I'm punctilious about such matters.'

'I'll second that,' said Gordon.

'The bag was on top of the table.'

'But it wasn't open?' said Hattie.

'Not open, no … but the clasp, I noticed, was not quite … quite snagged.'

'You mean?' asked Gordon.

'The clasp of the bag was sort of half-closed and half-opened.'

'Oh, yes,' said Gordon doubtfully.

'Sort of … loose, not what you'd call firmly snapped shut.'

'Oh, yes. And I suppose that in lifting the bag to put it back where it belonged, under the table, the clasp "somehow" failed.'

'Yes. It was very much along those lines.'

'Cut that stuff, Francis. You opened the bag?'

'Yes. And I knew at once. The words are horrible. They should have been consigned to the flames years ago. Why didn't you burn them, Mrs Taylor, that night when you first opened Belle Elmore's bag?'

'I wish I had. Those horrible, hateful words, they've never left me.'

'And you, Miss Prince?'

'I don't know,' said Hattie. 'In some strange way, it was as if the words belonged with the jewels, that they were meant to be together. I felt the whole thing was the most terrible warning.'

'Yes,' said Francis. 'But let's not forget. Make-believe is a wonderful thing.

We've been surrounded by it here, make believe all around us. We see, and we believe, but all may not be as it appears. That's why I looked in the handbag.'

'And?'

Francis sighed. Hattie looked in exasperation at Gordon, as if a cousin might hurry him up. Ethel looked from one to another, bemused at the unfolding of something that had resonated throughout her life. The silence, for that space, was intense, until Francis spoke.

'They're fakes.'

'What?'

'Fakes. When I first saw the jewels, I was as dazzled by them as you both were. But … I wasn't sure. If the mystery of the handbag was ever to be cleared up, I needed the opinion of a jeweller. There needed to be some sort of resolution, and what if these really were the jewels of Belle Elmore … it was a mystery that had to be solved. And then, I saw it.'

'Saw what?' Asked Gordon.

'The Rising Sun brooch. It was one of the reasons Belle's friends suspected Crippen had lied about her having gone to live abroad. You see, they knew that Belle would never have left her jewels behind, and when Ethel le Neve … another Ethel, I'm afraid, Mrs Taylor … when Crippen's mistress Ethel le Neve accompanied him to the Music-Hall Ladies' Guild charity ball held at the Criterion on 20th February 1910, Belle's friends noticed that she was wearing that most ostentatious item of Belle's jewellery, the Rising Sun brooch.'

'That was three weeks after Mrs Taylor took Belle's bag in mistake from Lyons Corner House,' said Gordon.

'Precisely.'

'But I don't understand,' said Mrs Taylor. 'What does it all mean?

'We may never know. It seems clear that Belle Elmore had reached a crossroads in her life. Her unhappy marriage with Dr Crippen, probably some male lovers who had abandoned her and gone in search of more youthful pleasures, her lack of success on the stage. I think she wanted out of it all. If the chance had presented itself, she possibly would have escaped to another country, just as Crippen tried to persuade everyone she had. However unsuccessful Belle considered her life, there is no doubt that she had accrued a considerable amount of money. From what I've read, in the days leading up to her murder she'd been visiting banks, trying to draw money out of her accounts, some of which her husband had no knowledge of. Whether he got wind of this, we don't know. I doubt it. If he'd suspected she was about to leave him, why would he have prevented her? He would have been free of her. No need for rat poison or whatever it was that finished her off.'

'Hyoscine,' said Gordon.

'No need to murder, no need to dismember her body. I think Belle's plans involved her jewels. These, she knew, would be crucial to her survival. And this is where my ideas run out, but for some reason, I think she had copies made.'

'But you don't know that all these jewels are fake,' interrupted Gordon. 'Some may be real. They certainly *look* real.'

'In all probability I think they are fake. What I think is almost certain is that Belle was planning something, some scheme in which the genuine jewels and the real jewels played an essential part. And … there is something else.'

'Something *else?*' asked Hattie. 'I don't think we could stand much more.'

'Oh, it's nothing, really,' said Francis, although his eagerness to come out with it was clear to all. 'It's just … Well, let me put it like this. What if Belle *wanted to get rid of the fakes?*'

'Wanted rid of them?' Mrs Taylor was wondering what other revelations were in store. 'You mean, it wasn't an accident at all? She meant me to take the wrong bag? You mean, she planned it? It never occurred to me, but … it seems amazing … Perhaps. You mean, she asked me to join her at the table because she noticed my bag and saw how it might work?'

'I'm not sure what I mean. But rearranging two handbags under a table, especially such large handbags with such sturdy handles … it's not beyond the realms of possibility, is it?'

Chapter Twenty Five

I

The final performance of *Forget-Me-Not* was as triumphant as the first. The crowd had slithered into the night, back along the now deserted moonlit pier into the old town, by the time Hattie and Gordon left the stage door for the last time. He felt extraordinarily moved by her very presence, hoping against hope that he would remember their friendship, those two extraordinary, unreal, weeks by the sea. It was such a cooling breeze, kind and listening.

'Thank you, love,' she said, moving the handbag about to shake his hand. 'Thank you for everything.'

'I won't forget,' he said. 'Dimple is waiting. He's waving to us.'

'We'd better wave back, then. Makes him feel wanted. We none of us know, do we?' she said.

He wondered after, at that moment and for years after, what she had meant.

'One last look,' she said. 'You look that side. I'll look this. Better safe than sorry.'

She thought for a second of an old song "We Parted On The Shore", mystified as to why it should come into her mind at that moment, but they parted, Gordon to the left and Hattie to the right, to gaze once more into, across, above that restless silence.

He heard the splash.

When they walked towards one another, she linked her arm into his. Their heights being so different, it was a lopsided arrangement, and silent, and the walk to the pier's entrance might have been a mile or more. The sound of their steps was all, below them hardly a murmur of sea, and their breath louder than all around, the old woman and the boy, strong and remembered in the night. Oh, the unspoken solemnity of that last departure from the pier, a carnival ended. After the ball is over, after the break of morn. After the dancers leaving, after the stars are gone. Many a heart is aching if you could read them all, many the hopes that have vanished, after the ball.

It was only when they reached the top of the pier that Gordon noticed the handbag had gone.

II

The wise know when it's over, the theatricals know the poisoned chalice of the last night party, the curtain down, the scenery dismantled, the make-up lazily wiped aside, the remnants of congratulation, the sense of there no longer being a reason for togetherness. For however long their contracts lasted, they clung to one another, survivors over a tireless sea, orphans of the theatrical storm. Oh, the wise know when it's time to creep away, to go quietly into the night, forsaking goodbyes.

The council, tempted to mark the end of the show's rejuvenating effect on the town's coffers with a bit of a do, thinks again, reminds itself that the cast is aged, two performances down that day, and old bones need rest. It would be cruelty to put on the bit of a do. By the time the performers have cleared the dressing rooms and packed their stuff, the theatre bar is deserted, the audience fled, any shred of excitement over and done with. It's a dark night but the moon, vicious and bright, ploughs a wrinkled way through the sea.

Gary has invited the company to a farewell drink at the Hotel de Paris in the Henry Blogg suite. Ravel and Rita are the first to arrive, eager to return to Hungary the next day, and not speaking or understanding a word of English, but making smiles do instead, and raising a glance as they laugh with Gary. Dorothy is fast on their heels, as summery as ever. Gary recognises her as a woman who keeps something in reserve when in the real world, a woman he would have liked to have known more. He sees how kindly she sits with Rita, how she makes the effort when Ravel tries to tell a joke, at least Gary supposes it's a joke because Dorothy throws her head back and sips at a sherry and Ravel seems pleased to have been even a little understood. It's a kindness that he suspects is typical of Dorothy. There is, nevertheless, a sadness about the Doll with a Dimple. To be saddled with that ridiculous sobriquet!

Dorothy sits quietly, thinking about another sherry. She had never been particularly fond of theatre folk, never singled them out as companions. Her ENSA years, all that up and downing across England, France too, and Belgium twice, and a spell at the Palladium – well, you don't do all that without having to fit in. ENSA and Bill, of course, that had meant something more. She might telephone Bill when she got back, she'd got the number, had looked at it often enough and thought, should I? She thought she might. Tomorrow, she'd be back at Mrs McNiece's, travelling by coach. She'd come to Cromer by train, but Heron Makepeace's unused return coach ticket had been found in his room and Mrs Freebody said it would be criminal to let it go to waste. She'd get her dad out of the old folk's home next week, same as usual, watch the independent television dramas at nine o'clock in Mrs McNiece's sitting-room, avoid cooking fish when she was allowed a go in the kitchen, sit in the park below the sign for the toilets.

She'd once met the writer Raymond Postgate in the park. A lovely man, and she'd taken a fancy to read one of his books, *The Ledger is Kept*. She realised how good it was to know someone who'd written things down. There was a sentence or two she had fixed on. One of the characters said 'It's a very hard thing to live … take your own decisions, do what you want with your life, or what you don't want, grow old, and know all the time that you are completely responsible and no one will save you from the results of anything that you do.'

Of course, she should have read that, known that, all those years before in ENSA. When Bill asked would she, she should have said yes, and if it hadn't been for Harry she might have. It might not yet be too late.

The Cromer Lovelies, thrilled to be so close to Gary, already having squirreled away stories around him that they would live on for years, were at their quietest. They had walked down the pier alongside Grenville and Elsie, who wished them on to an enjoyable party.

'We won't be attending, girls. Love to, but' Perry explained, 'I've got the chair.'

III

One of the girls said it sounded as if Perry had just been sentenced to death in Texas, the look on his face, and of course there was the difficulty of getting Elsie up to Gary's room, so Grenville and Elsie wouldn't make the party and were going back to the digs. Perry pushed the chair against the wind that had whipped across the town. He can't wait to leave this place. One of the few advantages of being behind the chair is that Elsie can't see his face. Never again, never ever again. It looms, closer and inevitable, the court appearance. He'll never forget that night.

If it hadn't been for Inspector Bellairs he'd be lost. He'd put all his trust in that man. Bellairs had come into the room when the two policemen had finished their questioning. He sent the younger officers out, sighed, sat opposite Perry, resting back into the chair. It was odd how Bellairs' face, not one you'd ever be much interested in, managed to express, what was it, a sort of regret?

'Got yourself into a bit of a pickle, Mr Grenville,' said Bellairs. He was clearly a master of understatement.

Perry felt his muscles relax for the first time since he'd tried running from the park, only to be winded when Sergeant Parker had brought him down in a flying tackle. The danger now was that Perry felt he might burst out crying at any moment, something he'd never have risked in the company of the other men.

'What can I say? It's a sort of weakness, I suppose, perhaps that's what you'd call it. But it's not something you'd want to try to explain, is it?'

'I suppose not,' said Bellairs. 'Apart from anything else, you're putting yourself in the way of danger, quite apart from breaking the law. Opening yourself up to blackmail, too, especially someone like yourself, in the public eye.'

'Oh, I don't think the public care tuppence,' said Perry, 'but it's bound to get into the papers.'

'You should have considered that before you acted so foolishly. You're elderly. 76 according to the charge sheet. Anyone would think you ought to know better. There are some pretty dubious characters haunt those places. They'd rob you and leave you bleeding on the floor. People who'd get a kick out of roughing up men like you.'

'Queers, I think, is the word your sergeant used.'

'He shouldn't have.'

'As for getting my name in the papers, they do say there's no such thing as bad publicity, but I'm starting to doubt it. A bit ironic, really. Soon as Elsie and I are back in the public eye, this happens. But the most bloody thing about it is what this will do to her when she finds out.'

'Does she have to?'

'What?'

'Does she have to know? Will you tell her?'

'Tell her?'

'It might be best. Sometimes they know, you know.'

'Who?

'Wives.'

'We're not married. I mean, we've been engaged for years, bloody years it's gone on. But we're not married, inspector.'

'Same thing. You've been together, shared your life. Sometimes the people we're closest to understand us better than we understand ourselves.'

'That wouldn't be difficult. I'm not sure it applies to Elsie.'

'It would be a way of finding out.'

'People kill themselves for less, don't they, when they're caught like this?'

'I think that would be overreacting. Sleep on it. It won't seem so bad in the morning.'

'I don't think I shall sleep tonight.'

'No. I don't suppose you will. This is probably the worst you'll feel.'

'Couldn't you just stop it? Just forget it? I've never pleaded before, but I'm pleading with you. It's not because of me, it really isn't. I'm not that much of a coward. But I fear for Elsie. She doesn't deserve to have to cope with this.'

'Mr Grenville. Let me be quite open with you.'

He couldn't be, of course. Why the hell had Blakiston and Parker arrested the man! Perhaps Blakiston thought arresting a homo was a feather in his newcomer's hat, and Bellairs had already deduced that Parker had a downer on such men. Dragging a man like Grenville through the ordeal of a court case, with all that implied about his reputation and relationships … when a few words of warning might have served everyone better. But all that came out of Bellairs was 'I don't approve of what you were doing …'

'God's sake, I wasn't *doing* anything.'

'…or what you might have been intending. The fact that it's against the law as it stands obliges me to officially disapprove. Perhaps the law is harsh. I know how difficult it can be for men of … your persuasion, but this isn't the time or place to discuss the rights and wrongs of it.'

'It's something I'd never do again, inspector. Not after this. I can tell you that.'

'That's as maybe, sir. At least, be careful in the future.'

'A caution, for God's sake …'

214

'No. There's no question of being unarrested, I'm afraid. You've been booked.'

Perry visibly slumped, tiredness taking over.

'There is something you can do, though,' said Bellairs. 'It's a way of mitigating the damage, but you have to plead guilty.'

'What?'

'Guilty. You'll still have to attend court. There's no way around that. It'll be a magistrate's court. What you'll need to do is to advise the court a few days before the case comes up that you've changed your address.'

'What? I'm sorry, my mind's fuddled.'

'Inform them in writing of a change of address. Make one up, if necessary, so long as it's a long way away.'

'What'll that do?'

'With any luck, keep you out of the local papers, for one.'

'God. Is that all?'

'Trust me,' said Bellairs. 'You're not the first person to go through this. It's the best you can do. With luck, you'll go down as a breach of the peace rather than importuning.'

'Oh God, that bloody word.'

'Do what I say,' said Bellairs.

'And if it doesn't work?'

'Oh, I think it should. And if it doesn't … everything fades with time, Mr Grenville. You're free to leave. We can get a car to drop you off at your digs.'

'Oh. That's kind of you, inspector, but I think a breath of fresh air … it must have stopped raining by now.'

Bellairs rose, opened the door, made way for Perry.

'Good luck, sir.'

Chapter Twenty Six

I

Last to arrive at Gary Rage's after-show get-together in the Henry Blogg suite of the Hotel de Paris were La Crème and his wife. Something about the organist had altered in the two weeks of forget-me-not-ing. In the unlikely event of his having worn corsets, he had loosened them. In future, mourners at his crematorium would leave the chapel with a jauntier step.

Young and inexperienced as Gary was, he was a perfect host. His guests realised, perhaps for the first time, how very little they knew of him, how he had kept himself apart throughout the time they had been together. If it wasn't for his impeccable manners, the ignorant might think him arrogant. They do not know him, do not see his kindly eye. Now, he knows the goodbyes need to be brief, cool rather than fervid. For a spell, he has been part of the music-hall of which he knew next to nothing, a world that is dying. He is intelligent enough to know that these weeks will find their place in his life, that time will tell, that his looks will fade, that popularity will come and go. He's been turned down for the following week's *Six-Five Special*. He doesn't mind; he thinks a lot of Adam Faith, as it happens. That's fine with Gary. He's part of a pattern, everything fits.

But things have been happening with his career since Monty signed him. It was Monty who put him up for the juvenile lead in a Frankie Howerd musical, *Mr Venus*, but Alan Melville, who apparently wrote it and then walked away from it, told him it would do his career no good if he got the part. Luckily, Gary didn't get it.

It was mere luck that Laurence Olivier was enjoying an autumnal break at Overstrand when he heard a fellow guest at his hotel rhapsodising about the young pop singer appearing down the road at Cromer Pier, how handsome, how beautifully spoken, how exquisitely the boy moved. It was probably no more than the absurdly exaggerated comments about second-raters Olivier had heard for years, but the fact that it was music-hall sharpened his interest. As a young man, Olivier had seen Hattie Prince on stage many times, and admired her from afar.

There was another reason why *Forget-Me-Not* interested him. John Osborne was writing a play, *The Entertainer*, about a broken-down music-hall comedian whose deep unhappiness reflected the death of music-hall itself, and subliminally, the death pangs of a sickly England. Olivier was determined to play the role, a role that would mark his move away from classical drama. His visit to Cromer Pier was, inevitably, a dark glasses affair, stealing into a seat at the back of the auditorium at the last moment. Nobody recognised him. Recognition, as Hattie and Enid knew, was a funny business at the best of times. People might glance and wonder, but how likely was it that Britain's greatest actor should take the trouble to sit through a show on Cromer Pier? Who knows what Olivier took away from that matinee of *Forget-Me-Not*?

The matinee had seen Dorothy Driscoll on top form, Ravel and Rita tangled themselves beautifully, Grenville and

Elsie made Olivier chuckle for all the wrong reasons and Parliamentary Pete for the right ones, and once again Olivier marvelled at Hattie Prince from afar, not wanting to go round after the show but slinking out into the early evening of the town because he knew instinctively that the illusion Hattie had created must not be broken. It was, however, the first time he had seen Gary Rage.

It was six months later that Olivier, recognising how something shone from the boy, arranged his engagement at the Old Vic. All the things that holidaymaker had said about the boy were true. The holidaymaker of course did not know that Gary spent much of his time at Cromer reading Schopenhauer. Watching Hattie as he stood alongside Gordon in the wings, he recalled Schopenhauer's words. 'Talent hits a target no one else can hit. Genius hits a target no one else can see.'

Gary Rage placed himself somewhere between the two.

II

The morning after the last night, breakfast at Mrs Freebody's was a gloomy affair, even more depressing than the breakfasts that had preceded it. Mrs Freebody, who has shown little interest in her guests' comings and goings during their stay, made sure of being at the front door, hoping for folding money as they vacated the premises.

Mrs Parliamentary Pete arrived before the cornflakes had got going to collect Mr Parliamentary Pete, presenting Mrs Freebody with a problem. She put Mrs Pete in the drawing-room beneath the photograph of Mr Freebody, who seemed to signal his disapproval of so chaotic a situation. When no tips were pressed into her hand, Mrs Freebody hurried into the abandoned rooms to see if donations had been left on bedspreads or bedside tables. She was disappointed. Checking the spoons, she could not account for two butter knives and a mustard-pot. She might as well not have been on duty when the parliamentarians left. They were so bound up in one another as they dithered on the doorstep that she felt invisible.

'You'll never believe what a success it was, May,' said Pete.

'Good. I'm glad for you.'

'I thought you might have come to see it, at least.'

'No. I've been fine. So long as you're happy, love. I'll take that bag.'

'No, I can manage. It balances the leg.'

'Taxi'll be here in a minute.'

They had escaped the porch, and stood at the gate of Mrs Freebody's kingdom, looking along the road, right and left, for the car that would take them away, take them back. The door closed silently behind them. Nothing was said, but both knew this must be how it felt to be let out of prison.

'Mind that bag,' said May. 'Sandwiches.' Her hand crinkled inside the bag she was holding. 'There's some cake for later.'

'You wouldn't believe the success,' said Pete.

'There's ham, with tomato.'

III

The coroner's report on the death of Heron Makepeace was discreetly tucked into the sidings of local newspapers. Harriet Wayworth's medical evidence threw no new light on the manner of his passing. Had he fallen or was he pushed? This, no one seemed to know.

Francis had sat through the proceedings. The fact that the death of Heron's mother had itself recently been the subject of an inquest was unusual, but not, in the opinion of the coroner, especially relevant. There was no doubt that Mrs Makepeace, obsessed with self-annihilation, had ultimately drifted off to sleep in the comfort of her own bed. The doctor who attended her was questioned about the bruising on her cheeks noted at the post-mortem, but had said this was nothing unusual. The pitiable sight of her weeping son in the courtroom drove any suspicions of foul play or smothering (remarkably close to mothering) from everyone's mind. It seemed curiously in line with his mother's death that Heron's death should also betray little evidence of what might had occurred.

Across the court, Francis saw the lifeboatman who had helped save Mrs Makepeace when she had been on the verge of being swept to sea. It was Mr Brenning, no longer a lifeboatman, but a fireman. A fireman who, very possibly (although no one mentioned it) had unexpectedly returned to Cromer as a member of the audience at the fire brigade's charity performance of *Forget-Me-Not*. What more natural than that he should come back to the town to support his colleagues and take the opportunity to reunite with the lifeboat crews he'd worked with. Francis had done a little investigation into the career of Mr Brenning, a distinguished member of the emergency services. Amongst his many accomplishments, Mr Brenning was a highly educated man, quite unlike the general public's image of the Henry Blogg-type lifeboatman. Mr Brenning had also written a slyly amusing little book about English grammar. Was there perhaps an echo of that style in the note that had fallen out of Heron Makepeace's pocket the night he vanished, the night that Mr Brenning had attended *Forget-Me-Not*? The note had read 'I no wot 'appened'. As Francis had remarked to Gordon at the time, it was the apostrophe that worried him.

Chapter Twenty Seven

I

Quite suddenly, the biggest surprise of his life, Henry is old.

Len drives the van back to Brighton, unloading the act and seeing Henry safely home. It's been a last hurrah for Henry, exhausted at the end of the run.

'It's yours,' he tells Len. 'If and when you want it, you can have the act. You could make a go of it.'

The thought had never occurred to Len. He doesn't consider it, not seriously, slightly embarrassed that Henry should say such a thing, give away something that had so much been part of his life.

'You can stay if you want,' Henry tells him. 'You'll have a place here. I showed them I could do it, anyhow. One more time, eh? And after all those years, running into Hattie again.'

'You never said. When did you work with her, then?'

'Oh, I never worked with her, lad. I was married to her.'

'You what?'

'I was Hattie's first husband.'

'You're kidding me.'

'Straight up.'

'*Married* to her? Why didn't you say? I mean, I don't think you said a word to her.'

'No. Not a word.'

'But she'd have known who you were, wouldn't she? Why didn't she speak to you?'

'Oh, she'd have known who I was, all right. Just thought it was better to keep quiet. It's fifty years ago since we met. I've changed a bit. But she must have known, of course she did, although I'd changed my name.'

'You could have said something to her, couldn't you?'

'Maybe. Funny thing is, she'd changed too. Little mannerisms here and there, things she's picked up over the years. We all change, lad. Your time will come.'

Len says goodbye, looks up the times of the train and leaves Brighton, changing at Manchester Piccadilly for Blackpool, and then on to Cleveleys. 'Alight for the Costa del Sol of the North!' cries the conductor, and it's bucketing down outside. Len chuckles along with everyone, gets off and heads for the promenade at the end of the High Street, turns right, walking at the side of the Irish Sea.

Mrs Grantley is waiting at the end of the walk, a good tea on the table beneath a damp cloth, her son and daughter here because they know it's special.

'He said he'd be here by two,' says her son, looking from the window.

'You daft beggar. You're more nervous than mum and me,' says his sister. 'He'll come soon enough.'

The rain falls fast now. Pelting, lashing in swathes across the promenade. Len turns his face to it, as he did when a child. In that tempest, done with almost as soon as it began, he's back on stage with Henry again, standing in the wings alongside

223

Gordon and the handbag-watching Hattie, standing beside Dorothy in the walkdown, opening the letter from his foster mum, reading it for the first time. Lost in the memories, he's surprised when he looks up and sees he's walked too far, past the house, so far along the furthest path at the end of Rossall that he's opposite Rossall School, away, as if it might be miles, across the scrub. It's all Gothic granite, seeming to belong to just as much an unreachable world as it had when he stared at it as a boy. There's the wall that divides, keeps him separated from privilege, the wall behind which he and Mrs Grantley's son did what young boys often do behind walls. He's soaking wet when the sun comes out, burning his face.

As it happens, the Grantleys saw him go past, at least saw a man tall as a giraffe walk past, and who walks this far along Rossall Beach on such a dirty day in late September? Mrs Grantley panics. Her son, who remembers Len and the times behind the wall, goes out from the house and looks along the path, calls to him, bellows against the weather.

'Len! Len! Where are you going, you daft sod? We're waiting for you, mate.'

Len turns, lifts his hand. He wouldn't have recognised the man, even when the man comes closer, walking towards him. It would be hard to say which of them moves the quicker.

II

Glynis returns to London, but only to pack another bag, all her bags, telling Monty it's been fun and Cromer had been just what she needed. Oh, to be away from London, where the old woman in the headscarf and the smell of the doss house about her and the glorious voice that rang through the darknesses of

Leicester Square can no longer be heard above the unthinking city. She telephones her mother in Ireland, telling her she, like Len, is coming home. She asks after the nuns, and there is news of Sister Agathe, older now, and visited with arthritis. It'll be a day or two yet, but Glynis is already there, walking up the slope towards St Gertrude's, an ear out for the ancient chuff of Father Brennan's motor car dragging up the hill behind her. Some old songs, remnants of the music-hall, memories of Piccadilly Lily, dribble through her mind as she goes past Riley's farm, the pig with the wonky ankles and rheumy eye still, you could say, keeping an eye out for her.

ENVOI

Hattie sits in her lumber-room, her sister opposite her. Enid takes off her hat, looks about for somewhere to put it, deciding at last on one of the many battered travelling trunks, a label that reads Australia, 1908. In the late September glow of sun that filters through the thick frump of velvet curtains, dust motes flicker about them, some of them almost a century old.

'Here's to us,' says Hattie.

Enid settles more confidently into the armchair. Little Tich sat there once, his feet never touching the floor, and George Robey, the room echoing of what once was. Ernest Lotinga once tried it on after Hattie had made meat paste sandwiches for supper. Happy Fanny Fields had sat there and cried because her career was over, and Hattie consoled her.

'Remember, dear, you're *Happy* Fanny Fields', Hattie had told her, but Fanny's pigtails continued to wobble as she sobbed on.

The glasses clink, Hattie stretching out across the space that divides them, and Enid, easing her feet from her shoes, reaches across to her sister.

'Over seventy years since we started, love,' Enid says. 'You and me, little Moira and Maisie. It was dad chose the names. What he wouldn't believe now!'

'He always said we were book-ends,' Hattie reminds her. 'Do you remember? Peas in a pod. We might have gone on like that for ever.'

'It didn't suit me,' said Enid. 'You had enough success for the two of us. I've been happy being part of it.'

'I'd never have done it without you.'

'No, I don't think you would. Who else would have put up with you? Who ever heard of having to be at a theatre four hours before they went on? I spent a lifetime fussing around you, making sure everything was right for you.'

'I was always a perfectionist,' said Hattie. 'You, too. But I never thought it would work.'

'It wasn't the first time,' said Enid. 'Remember the Camberwell Empire. 1910? You took ill.'

'Pleurisy.'

'You were in a bad way, I know that. You were out of it for months, and they'd already forgotten me, as if I'd never existed.'

'It would have finished me professionally, if you hadn't gone on.'

'Well, it was the least I could do,' said Enid. 'I knew your numbers, knew every move, every glance, every flick of your finger when you tapped a cigarette, and no one knew. They might have, you know. I mean, if you'd gone on as yourself, and then I tried to be yourself, they'd have known. But you'd already changed into a man. That made the difference, and what with us looking so alike, that made it possible.'

'You saved me. If I'd stopped working then, I might never have got back on my feet again. You got me into that nursing home under an assumed name. Nobody knew.'

'Remember Agate?'

'Agate?'

Of course she remembered! Enid knew she did. If Enid didn't remind her of him now she'd never dare bring his name up again.

'You must remember Agate, the great dramatic critic of his day, what he wrote about Hattie Prince in 1910?'

Hattie tipped her head to one side as if straining to recall.

'You're sure of the date, then?' she asked.

'Oh yes. June 1910. When I was Hattie Prince, and Agate thought he was writing about you.'

'I expect you're going to tell me what he wrote? Word for word?'

'Well, I'll never forget it. "The gods on Olympus look down in wonder on this most devastating of our feminine artistes, her trousers martially arranged, her waistcoats (beneath which beats the heart of the born troubadour) merely the badge of a theatrical mistress who has marshalled art to effect a legend. Miss Prince's art is an art in itself. Having no artifice, it pierces the onlooker, and we see in her a timeless understanding of the human predicament."'

'Fancy that,' said Hattie. She put her hand out to her sister. 'Your Mr Agate was right, dear. If you'd carried on, you'd have been as great a success as I was. I feel bad about it.'

'Oh, no.'

'Yes, I did and I do. It's not right that people should think he was writing about me when he was really writing about you.'

'It comes to the same thing. It's just that he came to see Hattie Prince the wrong week.'

'I mean … "The gods on Olympus" … no one ever wrote like that about me.'

'He would have, if he'd seen you, dear,' said Enid. 'And now, all over again, it didn't matter if it was you or me they were praising. No one will ever know. Why should they? Hattie Prince couldn't turn down headlining for Monty Desmond, could she? The chance of a final hurrah! Top of the bill, one more triumph. I knew you wanted to do it more than anything, that you'd never forgive yourself if you turned it down, but with you in that nursing home, just like in 1910 …'

'I was worn out, love, that's what it was. Thought I couldn't go on.'

'I knew what we had to do, knew I had to get you out of there, safe back here and get you looked after while I went off to Cromer and did it, became the great Hattie Prince all over again. And I knew your numbers, and no one knew the truth. I know it was me up there, but all I was doing was everything you would have done if you could. It was you they were loving. It was your success, Hattie, not mine. They never forgot Hattie Prince.'

'If you read it in a book, you'd laugh.'

'And then, the woman with a handbag,' said Enid. 'Ethel Braund. A lovely woman, she was, Hattie. Coincidences do happen, you know. It was as if the past was determined to meet up with the present to bring everything to a rounded conclusion, how that woman on holiday at Cromer was the woman who'd handed Belle Elmore's handbag over to Hattie Prince that night at Camberwell in 1910. Except, of course, that it wasn't Hattie she gave it to, it was me.'

'Twice deceived, poor woman. She thought you were me in 1910, and she thought you were me last week.'

Hattie set down her glass, sighed.

'The handbag,' she said. 'There's always been that bloody handbag.'

'Yes,' said Enid. 'Always the handbag. There was nothing I could do about it. It became a sort of curse that attached itself to me, a curse I had to keep to myself, safe, away from harm. That's why I took it to Cromer, to watch over it. But I've not brought it back, Hattie. It's gone.'

'How do you mean, love? Gone ?'

'Lost at sea. It was time for it to go. It was best.'

'And here we are. And no one need know any of it.'

'Oh, someone knows.'

'What?'

'A boy.'

'A boy. What boy? What did you tell him? After all the trouble, why on earth did you tell him?'

'Someone needed to know the truth, Hattie. I knew I could trust him. When we're both gone, it won't matter what he knows, and if he wants to tell the story, how could it harm us? It lends an enchantment, love. I think Gordon will keep our secret, and if one day he tells the story, it will be the better for coming from him. We can rest content. We've both of us had the greatest success that we could have hoped for. And when all's said and done, dear, we are *both* male impersonators.'

When all's said and done, aren't we all? Every man Jack, playing the game in the West, playing the game in the city? Leading the life that tells, flirting with Maude and Kitty? Strolling along the Strand, knocking policemen about? Well, we're not going home till a quarter to ten, 'cos it's our night out!